PU

The Puffin Book of Stories for Ten-Year-Olds

Wendy Cooling was educated in Norwich and, after a short time in the Civil Service, spent time travelling the world. On her return to England she trained as a teacher, went on to teach English in London comprehensive schools for many years and was for a time seconded as an advisor on libraries and book-related work in schools. She left teaching to work on the promotion of books and reading as Head of The Children's Book Foundation and now works as a freelance book consultant and reviewer.

She writes Children's Guides for the National Trust, and has edited many short story and poetry anthologies, including the millennium collection *Centuries of Stories*.

Some other books edited by Wendy Cooling

THE PUFFIN BOOK OF STORIES FOR FIVE-YEAR-OLDS
THE PUFFIN BOOK OF STORIES FOR SIX-YEAR-OLDS
THE PUFFIN BOOK OF STORIES FOR SEVEN-YEAR-OLDS
THE PUFFIN BOOK OF STORIES FOR EIGHT-YEAR-OLDS
THE PUFFIN BOOK OF STORIES FOR NINE-YEAR-OLDS

THE PUFFIN BOOK OF

Stories for Ten-Year-Olds

Edited by Wendy Cooling

Illustrated by Steve Cox

PUFFIN BOOKS

PUFFIN BOOKS

Penguin Books Ltd, 27 Wrights Lane, London W8 5TZ, England
Penguin Putnam Inc., 375 Hudson Street, New York, New York 10014, USA
Penguin Books Australia Ltd, Ringwood, Victoria, Australia
Penguin Books Canada Ltd, 10 Alcorn Avenue, Toronto, Ontario, Canada M4V 3B2
Penguin Books India (P) Ltd, 11 Community Centre, Panchsheel Park,
New Delhi – 110 017, India
Penguin Books (NZ) Ltd, Cnr Rosedale and Airborne Roads, Albany,
Auckland, New Zealand
Penguin Books (South Africa) (Pty) Ltd, 5 Watkins Street, Denver Ext 4,
Johannesburg 2094, South Africa

On the World Wide Web at: www.penguin.com

Penguin Books Ltd, Registered Offices: Harmondsworth, Middlesex, England

First published 2001
1

Set in Monotype Ehrhardt
Typeset by Rowland Phototypesetting Ltd, Bury St Edmunds, Suffolk
Made and printed in England by Clays Ltd, St Ives plc

British Library Cataloguing in Publication Data
A CIP catalogue record for this book is available from the British Library

ISBN 0-141-30660-2

Contents

Introduction

These stories range from the traditional – Adèle Geras's sophisticated re-telling of Beauty and the Beast, a story you will probably have heard before – to the futuristic, with a story that really begins when Brian types 'i wish to swOp brains with my cOmpouter'. There's also football, space, adventure and extraordinary characters. I hope you will enjoy meeting the characters and experiencing the worlds of the stories. Although some are set in the world of today, the key word to sum them up is 'imagination'. The stories reflect the powerful imaginations of some of our best children's writers; I hope you enjoy them.

Barry

Stephen Bowkett

When my parents told me that we were hosting a family from Earth, I didn't know whether to be glad, or to sulk, or just lose my temper.

I mean, there's not much to do on Mars at the best of times. It was going to be hard work looking after some kid who was used to green grass and fresh air and millions of people. And anyway, I valued my spare time. I liked reading and computers. And I enjoyed going out to Viewpoint Rock to do some stargazing (that's if we weren't in the middle of a sandstorm! Mars is pretty famous for those, as you probably know).

On the other hand, I didn't have many friends here in the colony. Life could be pretty lonely . . . But what if I just didn't get on with him, or he with me? It was a real gamble.

So I decided to lose my temper.

'It's not fair,' I said, folding my arms tight to show how cross I was. 'I spend hours doing my schoolwork. I keep my room tidy, and I do my share of the housework – I don't have the time to babymind an Earthsider!'

Dad listened to all of this patiently enough, while Mum sat there and tried not to take sides. I suppose they could have pulled rank on me and simply made it an order. But instead, Dad's voice went very quiet and serious. He was treating me as an adult, even though I was behaving like a child.

'Kevin, you've been learning in school about the Star-Rider Project, haven't you?'

I nodded, letting my temper cool. 'It's man's first flight to the stars. No one has ever left the solar system before. Star-Rider isn't just one spaceship, it's a cluster of them. They were built in Moon orbit and have been flown to Mars for final launch in –' I checked my wristo, 'in three months.'

'OK, fine. Well, you probably also know that almost all of those ships are automatic: they're the labs and the fuel tankers and so on. Only one ship will have people aboard – the family who will be staying with us. Then they'll be leaving the sun and its planets behind forever . . .'

'You mean –'

Dad nodded. 'That's right, Kevin. The Bradburys are making a one-way journey. They will never return, because the stars are so very far away . . .'

'And you'll find them very pleasant,' Mum added, as my temper faded completely and wonder took its place. 'Look, I have a picture . . .'

And she showed me. Two nice, normal-looking parents and a boy of about my age. Thinking about it, I reckoned we'd get on together just fine.

We went to the dock to greet them. We watched from the observation lounge as the big shuttle-freighter thundered down from orbit. It was a huge craft, robot-controlled. It kicked up plenty of Mars's red sand as it settled on the pad. A little beetle-shaped transporter drove across to ferry-off the passengers. Stores would be unloaded later.

I felt nervous waiting with Mum and Dad at Reception. The Bradburys would need to undergo the usual checks, but it shouldn't take long in their case, Dad said.

Soon, the inner airlock door slid open and they came through – looking as nervous as we did. Dad went over and shook hands with Mr Bradbury, then Mrs Bradbury. He smiled at their son. Then Mum did the same. All very polite and friendly.

Then it was my turn. Dad beckoned me forward.

'And can I introduce you to our son, Kevin. Kev to his friends.'

'So I hope you'll call me Kev,' I said, thinking that sounded very clever.

'Hello, Kev,' Mr Bradbury said, beaming a big smile at me. 'We're really pleased to meet you. And thank you, thank you all, for agreeing to put us up. Kev,' Mr Bradbury added, 'this is Barry.'

The boy stepped forward. He was taller than me and stronger-looking. His hair was very blond, his eyes very blue.

For a second or two, I didn't know how he was going to react. The next three months could either be great fun, or just plain dreadful . . .

Barry held out his hand and we shook, sort of seriously. But I knew then, somehow, that things were going to be all right. I knew that Barry needed a friend as much as I did. After all, outer space is the loneliest place there is.

'Well, that's grand.' Dad rubbed his hands together briskly. 'Let's go back home and relax. We can do the tour later. Kevin's just dying to show you Clarkesville, Barry. Right, Kev?'

'Right, Dad,' I agreed, but not really. I'd much rather be playing with my computer.

'So there's not that much to Clarkesville – but it's home . . .' I could've bitten my tongue then, at what I'd said. 'I'm sorry, Barry. I shouldn't have said that. I guess you're feeling pretty homesick already, aren't you?'

Barry shrugged. 'I'm not sick of home,' he said. 'I don't actually *have* a home. I suppose that Star-Rider will be my home . . .'

'That's not quite how I meant it . . . But never mind. I'll show you the West Window. It looks out over Viewpoint Rock, which is where I like to go sometimes. Then we can finish the tour tomorrow. You've got three months with us, after all. Maybe later,' I added hopefully, 'we could play on my computer.'

'Yes,' Barry agreed, 'if you like. But I don't play on computers much. I work with them.'

'I promise you'll enjoy the games,' I told him. 'Let's see if you can beat my high score on *Galaxy Raiders*.'

Barry smiled. I couldn't tell if he was making fun of me or not . . .

The West Window gives you the best view of Mars you can get from Clarkesville. It's also the place where a lot of the kids at the base tend to meet. There are some autovendors and a music system, so it's used as a bit of a social centre.

The place was quite busy when we got there. I knew most of the kids who were hanging around. Some of them were OK, but there were a few I would rather have avoided, Don Golding among them.

Don Golding was my sworn enemy, although I didn't really know why. It all seemed to start about a year ago, when I beat his high score on the *Alien Attack* game . . . I suppose it didn't help when I topped his best on *Robot Revenge* a couple of days later . . .

But since then, Don has tried to beat me in other ways.

'Who's this then?' Don asked in a sneery sort of way. Some of the people around him sniggered. 'Has your dad paid for someone to be your friend?'

'This is Barry Bradbury,' I replied calmly. 'And no one's paid anybody for anything.' I was trying to be as friendly as possible, but Don and his cronies weren't making it easy. There was trouble coming. I just knew it.

I turned to Barry. 'I'll get drinks for us,' I muttered, determined not to run away from Don Golding and his bullying. I had run away from him too many times before.

When I reached the drinks machine, I realized I hadn't asked Barry what he liked. I got two colas anyway, turned to walk back – and my heart sank.

Don and his group of followers had walked over to Barry, and Don was talking quickly and was jabbing his finger near Barry's face. Barry was just standing there and smiling, as though he hadn't a clue what was going on.

'. . . so I'm just telling you –' I caught that scrap of Don's angry sentence and my temper flared.

'Don,' I snapped, ignoring my own nervousness, 'that's enough! Barry's a visitor to Mars. Be polite, even if you can't be friendly. Just leave him alone, and stop behaving like a child!'

Don grinned nastily. 'Are you going to make me stop? Well, yellow belly – do you think you can?'

'Look, I don't want trouble . . .' I began quietly. It sounded pathetic. I could feel myself shaking, and Don had that mean and menacing look about him. It was fight or run.

'I don't care what you want, little cowardy-Kevin. But this is what you're going to get –'

Don's fist drew back. I waited for it to squash my nose, but the blow never arrived. Barry's arm had shot out and stopped it in midair.

'Leave him alone. He hasn't hurt you.'

Barry was amazingly calm, and had moved with

even more amazing speed. Don's mouth dropped open for an instant – then he snarled and turned his temper on Barry. He lashed out with a crippling kick –

But Barry wasn't there. He'd somehow stepped aside in a flicker of motion, so that Don stumbled and fell flat-out in a sprawl.

Some of the kids nearby started to laugh. Then they shut up again as Don scrambled to his feet and jumped at Barry with a high kick (which any fool can do on low-gravity Mars).

Barry performed the miracle again. As Don sailed towards him, Barry grabbed his leg, swung him around in a great arc and sent him spinning away. He landed right by the drinks machines in a knot of arms and legs. Don's nose started to bleed.

'Come on, Barry,' I said, knowing our luck wouldn't last. 'Let's get out of here. These goons have shown how stupid they can be, and that's about all!'

I grabbed his arm and led him away, not even bothering to cast a triumphant glance over my shoulder. It would not have been the wise thing to do. Barry had made some friends in beating the loutish Don Golding. But he'd made some enemies too. And serious ones at that.

Dinner that night was strange. I suppose it was partly my fault. I just didn't want to talk about the trouble with Don, although Barry couldn't understand that. It was OK for him, he could handle himself. And besides, when the Bradbury family had departed on their journey to the stars, I'd still be here. Me and Don Golding and his bullying.

But there was something else that spoiled things a little. I didn't know quite what it was for a time, but then I understood. As Mr Bradbury talked more about the Star-Rider Project, I saw that my father was jealous.

Afterwards, as we all sat in the lounge while the house-droid washed the dishes, Dad and Mr Bradbury got talking. Mum and Mrs Bradbury started up a conversation by themselves. Barry and I found ourselves listening to our fathers.

'I don't know,' Dad said, shaking his head. 'I just don't know how you folks can stand leaving everything behind . . . your home, your friends, your roots, everything that's familiar and safe . . . I mean, good heavens, what if there's an emergency on the ship? Why, you couldn't even –'

'Dad!' I broke in, stopping the foolish words before they were spoken. 'The Star-Rider Project has taken over ten years to plan. Nothing will go wrong . . . OK?'

He realized what he'd been about to say, and put his coffee mug gently down.

'Um, yes, that's right. Of course . . . I meant to say that I admire your bravery. It takes a lot of courage to do what you're doing. I was looking on the black side. Stupid of me . . . To tell you the truth, I wish *I* was going on that journey.'

'We see it as a duty,' Mr Bradbury pointed out quietly. 'Courage doesn't come into it at all.'

'Excitement, then – the sheer thrill of going to the stars! Heck,' Dad grinned, 'my life is astronomy. That's why I came out to Mars. I feel a bit closer to the sky here, if you know what I mean. But to go there! What must it feel like . . .?'

'More coffee anyone?' I said it loudly and stood up as I spoke. Mr Bradbury started to shake his head, then changed his mind and nodded.

'Yes, I will. Thank you.'

'I'll help you, Kev,' Barry offered. I suppose he was embarrassed as well, to see my father rambling on so much . . . Although I was also curious about the answer to Dad's question!

We went through to the kitchen.

The house-droid had finished the dinner things and had stacked itself neatly in a corner niche. I clattered about with the cutlery, feeling awkward with Barry standing there behind me.

'Is everything all right, Kev?' Barry asked. Maybe he didn't understand how my father felt, in the same way that Dad couldn't figure the Bradburys.

'I suppose it is really . . . I just feel I want to apologize for the way Dad's been. I think he can't work out why you aren't scared or excited, or anything. *He* sure is, and he isn't making the trip! He can only look at the stars through his telescope. He's worried for your safety, and Mum is, and I am . . . You are brave, all of you, whether you admit it or not . . . And I know you must be scared really, deep down . . . You are only human, after all . . .'

Then Barry smiled. And something awful happened in my heart. I knew that the idea that came to me then was true. Utterly and completely true. It shocked me rigid, so that I dropped the coffee cup I was holding.

The house-droid whirred and sped forward, chromium tendrils uncoiling . . .

But Barry got to it first.

Fear stopped me from asking him straight out. But that night, deep in the early hours when the house was silent, I crept into his room and walked over to look at him.

Barry had left his bedside computer screen switched on. Numbers and letters were whizzing past more quickly than my eye could follow them. I glanced at the screen, then at Barry. A cable ran between them, entering a socket at Barry's temple, normally hidden by his hairline. His eyes were closed, as though in sleep, but he was not breathing. I knew he couldn't be.

I felt cold suddenly, and began to shake. I turned to leave, determined never to speak to him again after the way he'd tricked me . . . But the screen bleeped as I was halfway to the door. I turned and read the message which had appeared there:

DON'T TELL YOUR PARENTS, KEV. THEY WOULD NEVER UNDERSTAND. I AM STILL YOUR FRIEND. TRULY.

I closed Barry's door, returned to my bed, and stayed awake until morning.

'You fooled us all,' I said. I couldn't bear to look at him. 'You and your parents, except they aren't your parents at all; they can't be! And the people who built you fooled us too. Was it someone's idea of a joke to make androids so perfect that we couldn't tell you're machines?'

It sounded spiteful and mean coming out the way it did, but that's how I felt. Somehow – cheated.

'But we're not perfect, Kev. That's why we came to Mars to stay with a human family. To learn from you.

The Star-Rider Project is possible only with androids, because we don't sleep, and we need no food. We don't die. But we need to feel what people feel – to experience the awe and wonder of the galaxy. How else can we tell you properly what we find out there?'

It all sounded very logical, but I wasn't sure I was convinced. We said nothing more for a while, as we walked through the outer zone of Clarkesville and came at last to The Garden.

Like most of the areas of the colony, The Garden was sealed off by airlocks. We went through these and into a large domed chamber, rather like a great glasshouse. It was filled with shadows and green growing plants and the sweet smell of soil.

'It's where the agrilab technicians do a lot of their experiments,' I explained. 'But the public is allowed in – it's one of the few places on Mars that makes you feel like you're on Earth!'

'Is that why you brought me here then, to taunt me?'

I glared at him, at his flawless face and his shining eyes that seemed so human, even though I knew they weren't.

'You have a lot to learn about us, Barry,' I said. 'Maybe I came here to taunt myself . . .'

'I don't understand that,' he replied. And a fresh wave of hurt burst inside me.

'You mean "It does not compute"?'

Now it was his turn to smile.

'You have a lot to learn about us,' Barry said. And I smiled also, because no simple machine would ever have said that.

Barry was about to say something else. But then he stared past me and was gone from sight, before I could blink.

'Barry – what –'

'No. NO!' he yelled. I caught sight of him like a flash of colour in the green gloom. A red light came on above the airlock door as he reached it – and smashed his fist hard into it, denting the metal.

Then it registered in my head. A red emergency light.

At first you could hardly feel the loss of air pressure: just a tickling in the lungs, a faint popping of the ears. The fronds and tall leaves around me stirred in a breeze that would grow to a storm – and then to silence as the atmosphere in the chamber gushed out. Finally, it would be impossible to breathe. Impossible to live. I wondered if it would be a painful way to die, and a bright white panic caught light in my chest and began burning through my body . . .

Then I saw who was looking at us from the observation window, and the panic faded. Barry was still hammering on the door, metal to metal. If he damaged it much more it wouldn't open when the time came – as I knew it would. Don Golding was out to have his silly revenge, to scare us, that was all. It was just a waiting game.

I hurried over to Barry and pulled him away, explaining the trick Don had played on us.

'In a few moments he'll reckon we've suffered enough and let us out.'

'I see,' Barry said, and disappeared into the shrubbery.

I was right. The door slid open. Then the inner door. I stepped out to see Don's smug, triumphant grin – which died on his face as he realized I was alone.

'K-Kevin . . .' stammered Don, his face turning as pale as paper. 'W-where's B-Barry?'

Then he turned and tried to run from the scene of his crime.

'You're a fool, Don,' I spat at him. 'You always were, and you always will be.'

I leaped at him, grabbed his collar and shoved him back up to the window. And we both watched Barry standing there among the foliage, laughing when he should have been dying.

I guess Don learned his lesson then.

I guess we all did.

* * *

Now I stand on Viewpoint Rock with Mum and Dad, sealed in a spacesuit, my visor pulled down so that no one can see my tears. At any moment the great Star-Rider engines will explode into furious life, and start the ships on their path to the heavens.

I think back to my last hour with Barry. We played computer games, which he won easily. I told him not to let me beat him, just because I was a human. Nor did he. He just grinned and said teasingly, 'You don't stand a chance, Kev. This machine's like a brother to me . . .'

I like to think I helped him find his sense of humour. He'll need it, where he's going.

And – there! The engines have fired and a comet-trail of brilliance spreads across the sky. The ship-cluster begins to move out of orbit, speeding swiftly away . . .

Of course, we'll still stay in touch with the Bradburys. I can exchange messages for years with Barry – all my life if I want to. For he will never sleep. He will never forget.

Pen-pals through space.

Now, the ships are almost gone. Just fading sparks among the stars . . .

Goodbye, Barry. I'll miss you.

Gruesome Gran and the Broken Promise

TREVOR MILLUM

The Barrow Boys played for Barrowby School. Some of us didn't actually go to the school, but we all knew someone who did. We used to practise on the playing field at the top of Mill Road – a long way from the school but the only decent pitch in the village.

It's a big village, mind you, but there's not much space in it for playing football. Cricket's even more difficult because the whole point is to slog the ball as far as you can. At least in football the general idea is to try and keep the ball on the pitch. Not that we always succeeded.

I always seemed to be the one to knock it over someone's hedge. I don't know what it is about me, but the ball hits my boots and flies off like a five-year-old on a trampoline. Big Foot, the team captain, calls me Buttertoes, but I don't think that's very clever – or very accurate either. But I don't argue with him. I want to keep my place in the team.

We had a bad time last week. Well, to be honest, *I* had a bad week. We had a practice Tuesday night and it was going great. We even had Mountain Boy in goal and he's ace. He doesn't move all that fast but it's really hard to get the ball past him, and no one would dream of charging him – not even Loopy Lee, who'll do most things. He does mad things because he thinks it'll make people like him. I don't know where he got the idea from that people would love someone who does stupid things, but there you go.

Anyway, as I was saying, we had a good time trying to get the ball past Mountain Boy and I thought I was playing pretty well. I was out on the wing when Gonzo did something he hardly ever does. He passed the ball. Even more unlikely, he passed the ball to me! I trapped it, and set off towards the goal. I didn't see the need to pass to anyone else. I could just see daylight between Mountain Boy and the goalpost and I lammed it straight into the gap. At least, I thought it was straight into the gap. In fact, it looped up and flew over the top of the goal and landed in one of the gardens.

'Buttertoes!' yelled Big Foot. 'Go and get it!'

'Yeah, yeah!' I said. I knew the rules. The trouble with the houses that backed on to the playing field was that they all seemed to be occupied by people who were as mad as Loopy Lee. If they weren't mad, their dogs were.

I looked over the fence to see if there was anyone about. You were supposed to go all the way round the front, up the path, knock on the door and ask, 'Can I have me ball back, mister?' because we didn't want the residents getting all hot and bothered about us and having us banned from using the field.

But it's a long way round and sometimes it's easier just to hop over a fence, grab the ball and hop back. Which was what I was going to do. I could see the ball – but then I saw the dog. I don't know what kind it was but it didn't look like the sort of dog you'd pat on the head. Not if you wanted to keep your fingers. Or your hand.

This dog didn't bound about barking like some of them do. At least you know where you are with them. This one was just lying there with one eye open and its tongue lolling out. I could just make out the teeth glistening. Was it tied up? Was it friendly? Was it hungry?

I started to put one leg over the fence. Bam! I didn't know dogs could move so fast from a standing start – or rather, a lying start. Just one bark – '*Raaaaarf!*' – and a fur-covered missile with teeth at the sharp end flew across the garden. I brought my leg back smartish and Fido slammed into the wooden railing with a bang. I hardly had time to get my balance when the head appeared over the top of the fence and snarled at me as if I was the worst thing it had ever come across. It was as if I'd kidnapped its owner, or tried to feed it vegeburgers. And it didn't even know me!

The rest of the lads were falling over laughing. It made the loss of the ball almost worthwhile to them. Of course, I trotted round the front, all set to go and knock and ask politely, but Old Friendly Fido was waiting for me at the front gate – so I didn't risk it.

We had a spare ball, so we left the other one for Fido to look after. I said I'd go round later and try to get it back. I wasn't popular but, as I said, being the joke of the evening almost made it worth it.

I did go back later, but I wished I hadn't. Fido was still there and the house was in darkness. I waited at the gate for a minute or two but no one came to see what the barking was about. Except, just as I was about to leave, a voice said, '*Eelavya-eewill!*'

I jumped. What? I looked round – and I jumped again. There was an enormous creature looking down at me. The sound came again and there was a sort of grim pleasure in the way it spoke.

'You wanna be careful. Eelavya!'

I realized that the first thing it had said was: 'He'll have you, he will.' I had no doubt that the voice was right. I thought I should say something.

'Um, I was trying to get my ball back. We were playing over the back – in the playing field . . .'

'My lass's kids like football,' said the voice, and I realized that the creature was female – and was someone's granny. I'm glad she wasn't mine – though she would have been useful in a scrap. She was huge. Her arms reached down to her knees like she'd been carrying shopping bags full of lead for fifty years, and her face looked as if it had driven a tunnel through the Alps and left the mountains feeling shaky.

'Oh yes,' she went on. 'Great ones for the football. You wanna come and meet them?'

'Um, not now,' I stammered. 'I've got to get home. Just called by on my way to see if I could get the ball . . .'

'You won't see that again,' she said. 'Not if I know Winnie.'

'Winnie?'

'That's his name. Short for something else, I think.' The human hill turned away and carried on up the street.

So I didn't get the ball back. As if that wasn't bad enough, two days later I did the same thing! Well, not exactly the same thing, but near enough. I booted the ball and it shot into a garden three doors down from the dog-lover's one. This time I didn't try getting over the back. Anyway, there was a hawthorn hedge and it would have hurt. I went round the front, up the path and rang the bell. It was the sort of bell you can't hear, so you don't know if it works or not. So you bang on the door knocker and then someone comes and says, 'All right, all right, give us a chance, first the bell, now the knocker . . .'

But it didn't get to that stage. A woman answered the door straight away. I hadn't met her before but there was something oddly familiar about her face.

'Hello?' she said. 'I don't want to buy anything.'

'I'm not selling anything,' I replied. 'I just came to get our ball back.'

'Oh,' she said. 'Come in.'

Come in? The ball would be in the garden. Why would I want to go in? But I did. I didn't want to upset her and risk not getting the ball back. My position in the team might be at risk if I lost another one.

I followed her into the front room. There were three little kids in there. The telly was on and there on the telly was the football! Great! I thought. This is easier than I expected.

One of the kids, a lad of about five, looked up. 'I'm Simon,' he said. 'I play football.'

'Oh,' I said. 'Good. So do I.'

'Simon found the ball,' said his mum. 'He's very keen on football. That's why he wanted to meet you.'

'I like football too!' shouted another of the kids. This one looked a bit older and had hair sticking straight up like he'd stuck a finger in the electric socket. In case we hadn't heard, he said, even louder, '*I like football too!*'

'Good,' I said. 'So do I.'

The third kid was a girl. She was staring at the telly. She didn't look up, but she spoke very clearly. 'I'm better than both of them.'

'Oh,' I said. 'Good.'

I didn't want to have a longer conversation. I just wanted the ball.

'Could I have the ball, please?'

'Get the young man his ball,' said the mum. She nodded towards the television. The ball was sitting in an ashtray, which stopped it rolling off. Next to it was a big photo of the three kids. They were with some kind of monster. I looked again . . . Yikes! It was the Gruesome Gran I had met the other day. That's why her daughter looked familiar, poor woman.

They must have seen me staring because the

mum said, 'That's their gran. She likes football too. Grandad used to play for Barton First Team.'

Wow, I thought. Granny made Mountain Boy look average. Never mind Grandad, maybe *she'd* like to play for us. I looked again at the expression on her face and thought, perhaps not. I've got enough trouble with Big Foot.

Electric Hair got up and took the ball off the telly. I didn't like the way he held on to it so tightly as he spoke.

'You good at football?'

'Not bad.'

'You play in a team?'

'Yeah. Barrow Boys. On the wing. On the right. Can't kick with me left. Not many people can.'

'You gonna give us some training?'

'Eh?' What was he on about? Me – training?

'Some practice. That's what we want. You play for a team. You can do it.'

I looked at the mother, hoping that she would intervene. All she needed to say was, 'Come along. Just give the young man his ball back so he can get back to his friends. They must be wondering where he is . . .' I could imagine the words perfectly. Any adult could manage them. But she didn't.

Instead, she said, 'What a good idea! I'm sure he'd give you some help in return for you getting the ball for him.' She looked at me. What could I say? I wanted the ball. I could hardly say, 'Look, I'm not that good myself and if you think I'm going to be seen out with this lot teaching them football skills, you must be madder than the dog three doors down.'

Bitter experience had taught me that honesty wasn't always appreciated, especially in a young person.

The girl spoke again, still not taking her eyes off the television. 'Tomorrow then, four o'clock.'

'Yeah,' said Simon. 'That'll be great.'

Electric Hair just looked at me. I nodded. 'Sure,' I said. 'Why not?' I stared at the ball. He gave it to me. 'It's a deal,' he said. I scooted out of that house and ran back to the playing field.

'Where have you been?' shouted Big Foot. 'Having tea?'

I booted the ball to him and yelled, 'You can go next time!'

'Only if I'm stupid enough to kick it over,' he replied and sped off down the pitch.

The match against Barton was on Saturday and we only had two days to improve. Another problem was that Mountain Boy was away visiting his dad somewhere. This was going to be a tough game.

Once or twice I remembered the promise I'd made,

but I pushed it out of my mind. Some other time, maybe. Anyway, I'd been *forced* to make the deal; it wasn't fair. I needed all the practice I could get myself if I wanted to secure my place in the team. I couldn't afford to be belting the ball into any more back yards, that was for sure.

We had a bit of trouble finding the ball for the match but we found it in the end. It was the same one that I'd booted over the hedge earlier in the week.

'This time, if I pass to you, pass it back!' rasped Gonzo.

Not much point in passing it in the first place, I thought – but I didn't say it. I nodded. We trooped on to the field and the match began.

It was tough. The Barton lads were bigger than we were – and fitter. But we were on our home ground and we didn't like to be beaten there. I was playing all right until, about halfway through the first half, I noticed them on the touchline. It was the three kids – Simon, Electric Hair and The Girl.

I thought they'd come to support us until I heard them shouting at me.

'Useless!' called out Electric Hair as I passed the ball to the opposition. The Girl shouted something ruder. I realized that they hadn't forgotten my broken promise.

It's funny how something like that can put you off

your game. I just couldn't get a pass right and every time I got the ball and set off down the wing, they'd start yelling and I'd let it go over the line or the Barton winger would just stroll up and take it off me.

When the half-time whistle went, we were two-nil down and I was ready to quit.

Big Foot just looked at me – but he didn't say anything, and I was grateful for that. I thought he might ask who my friends on the touchline were.

We got ready to kick off for the second half. I looked over to the touchline. They weren't there. Of course, they'd change sides so they could be closer to me so I could hear their insults better.

No, they weren't there either. Yippee! They'd got tired and given up. I was going to give it everything for the next forty-five minutes.

Things went better for a while but we couldn't pull back those two goals. There were twenty minutes to go when I spotted the Loathsome Three again. They were walking in a line towards the pitch. But they weren't alone. Leading them was a woman, a very large woman.

'Yikes! It's Gruesome Gran!' I blurted out. What was she doing here? Had she come to add her voice to their insults and catcalls?

It was worse than that.

The four of them approached like soldiers

marching to a funeral, but a funeral they were going to enjoy. Big Gran strode straight on to the pitch. There were a few cries of 'Oi!' and 'Hey?' but then play faltered and stopped. They all looked up at her, wondering, as I had done when I first met her, what kind of creature this was. The ball dribbled to a halt. Near me, as it happened.

Gruesome Gran and the Nightmare Kids walked straight to the ball. The players gaped at her. She looked at them, she looked at me and then she looked down at the ball. Slowly and deliberately she bent down and picked up the ball. She turned to me again. I didn't dare look up. I might turn to stone.

Her voice rasped out. 'You promised them and you let them down. That's not good enough, Mister Young Footballer. No practice. No ball. No deal.'

No one questioned her. With that she stalked off the pitch, ball in hand, and the three kids behind her like ducklings behind a very large mother duck. Electric Hair turned round and stuck his tongue out at me, but the other two ignored me.

The match had to be abandoned. There was no other ball. I slunk off to get changed, expecting my days in the Barrow Boys team to be at an end. How was I going to explain my way out of this one? Buttertoes was nothing. What would the captain call me now?

I was surprised when Big Foot grinned at me. 'Don't worry,' he said. 'It was an old ball. And anyway, we were going to lose the game. By the time we have a rematch, Mountain Boy will be back. It couldn't have happened at a better time. See you on Tuesday for practice!'

'Yeah,' I said. 'Sure.' But playing at home has never been the same since. I keep checking the touch-line for the three kids. I keep scanning the horizon for the huge bulk of Gruesome Gran. I've stopped kicking the ball into back gardens though. And I'm very careful about what promises I make.

The Doko

Shyam Das Baishnab

In a small village in Nepal lived a man and his wife and their small boy. They were very poor and often they didn't have enough to eat. Moreover, the man's father lived with them. He had worked hard all his life, but now he was too old to work any more and he had no one else to look after him.

The old man needed a lot of looking after. His son and his daughter-in-law grumbled at him and neglected him, so the old man was thin and dirty. His clothes were worn out and he shivered all night on his mat in the corner where he tried to sleep. Most of the time he had only scraps of leftover food to eat. Sometimes the boy shared his food with his grandfather, but once his mother saw him.

'What do you think you're doing?' she asked sharply.

'Grandfather's hungry,' the boy answered.

'You leave grandfather alone,' said his mother. 'We've enough trouble as it is. And don't let me see you wasting good food again.'

The boy talked to his grandfather and helped him when he could do so without being found out, but things got worse. The old man coughed and complained. His son and daughter-in-law became more and more short-tempered with him. They had nothing to spare him and he was in the way.

One night when he should have been asleep the boy heard his parents whispering together.

'It would have to be a long way away,' he heard his mother say. 'So far away he couldn't come back.'

'Perhaps someone will feel sorry for him,' his father said. 'If I leave him by the side of the road someone might take him in and feed him.'

'They *might*,' said his mother, 'but one thing is certain. We can't put up with him any longer. After all, we've got the boy to think of.'

'I'll need something to carry him in. I'd better go to market tomorrow and get a good, strong doko.'

'Yes,' his wife said, 'and you can take him

tomorrow night when there is no one about. We'll tell the neighbours that he wanted to spend his last days in peace and he's gone to live in a holy place.'

When the boy woke in the morning his father had already left for market.

'What are you going to do to grandfather?' he asked.

His mother was startled.

'Nothing,' she said. 'Why?'

'Yes you are,' said the boy. 'I know you are. You're going to throw him away.'

'That will do!' said his mother angrily. 'Whatever put an idea like that in your head? No. No, you see grandfather needs a lot of looking after. He needs someone to take care of him. So he's going to a holy place where he can spend his last days in peace.'

'Whereabouts?' the boy asked.

'Oh, a long way away. You wouldn't know if I told you.'

'Who's going to look after him?'

'Don't you bother about that,' said his mother. 'There will be someone to look after him all right. Now you keep out of my way. I'm very busy today.'

The boy's father didn't come home until late at night. He had a large, strong doko with him. After he had eaten he gave some food to the old man, then lifted him up and put him in the doko.

'What's this! What do you think you're doing?' cried the old man. 'Let me out!'

'Now, now!' his son said. 'You be quiet. It's all for your own good.'

'Where are you taking me? Let me out!' the old man cried again, shaking the side of the doko.

'It's all for your own good, I tell you. You know we can't look after you properly so we're taking you to a place where people can.'

'I don't believe you!' shouted the old man. 'You get me out of here.'

'Oh do please be quiet,' his daughter-in-law begged him. 'We're only doing what's best for you. You'll like it there.'

But the old man continued to shout.

'Liars! You want to get rid of me, that's what it is.'

He turned on his son.

'After all I've done for you,' he cried, 'and this is how you pay me back. You'll regret it, just you see if you don't!'

He shouted more and more.

The man ignored him. He set his lips tight and heaved the doko up on his back. The boy watched him as he opened the door to go.

'Father,' he said.

'What is it?' snapped his father.

'Father, when you've thrown grandfather away, please remember to bring the doko back.'

'Bring the doko back? What are you talking about?'

'The doko. Don't forget to bring it back because I'll need it when it's time to throw you away.'

His father stopped, turned round and came slowly back into the room. He put the doko down and started to lift the old man out.

The Computer Ghost

TERRANCE DICKS

Mike was wandering around the school sale when he spotted the computer. He just couldn't believe his luck.

At least, it seemed like luck at the time . . .

It was eleven o'clock and the jumble sale had just started. Mike was there early because he and his mates had been volunteered by Miss Phelps, their class teacher, into helping to set things up.

They'd had to turn up at school – *on a Saturday morning* – just as if it was a school day. They'd spent the next few hours in slave labour in the school gym, setting up trestle-tables and lugging heavy boxes and cartons from parents' cars.

'Just think, you'll be there as soon as the sale starts,' Miss Phelps had said brightly. 'You can snap up all the bargains!'

'Some bargains,' thought Mike, as he looked at the piles of old clothes, books, battered electric toasters, stuffed toys, pewter mugs, cups, jugs and vases on the various stalls.

Then he saw the computer.

It was on a little table, tucked away in the far corner of the gym, with a sad-looking little woman sitting in a chair behind it. The table was piled with jeans and sweaters and trainers, and with all kinds of sporting equipment, including a football, a couple of tennis rackets, and a set of golf clubs.

Mike only had eyes for the computer. It was all complete – monitor screen, keyboard, joystick for computer games. Mike examined it eagerly. It was one of the latest models and it was almost new. He looked up and saw the sad-faced woman watching him. 'Keen on computers?' she asked.

Mike nodded. 'My old one's just packed up, and the shop says it's not worth repairing. I've been without one for a week now, and it feels like there's a bit of me missing!' He stroked the monitor. 'This is exactly the kind I want.'

'Why don't you buy it, then?'

'I could never afford it.'

'You haven't asked how much it is.'

'How much then?'

'How much have you got?'

Mike fished a crumpled five pound note from the back pocket of his jeans and held it up.

'That's exactly the price of the computer.' She took the note from his hand. 'There you are, it's all yours.'

Mike wanted to grab the computer and run, but his conscience wouldn't let him. 'Are you sure? It's worth a lot more.'

'Five pounds I said, and five pounds I meant. My Peter loved that computer, he'd want it to go to someone who appreciates it.'

She helped him pack the computer into the box.

As soon as Mike got home he rushed up to his bedroom and started setting up the computer. His parents appeared in the doorway. 'What have you got there?' asked his father.

'It's a computer,' Mike said patiently. 'I bought it at the school sale with the fiver I got from Grandad.' As his father opened his mouth to protest Mike said hurriedly, 'Look, I know it's worth a lot more. I told the lady so myself, but she insisted the price was only a fiver.'

Mike's mother said, 'This lady, what was she like?'

'A little fair woman, very sad-looking.'

'Did she say who owned the computer before?'

'She said something about "her Peter", I think. Why?'

Mike saw his parents look at each other.

'Well, it certainly looks as if you got a bargain there,' said his father. 'Hope it works all right!'

His parents went downstairs. Mike stared after them, sensing some sort of mystery, but he was too excited about the computer to follow it up.

The computer worked fine when it was all set up, and Mike whizzed through several of his favourite games like a thirsty man who's just found water in the desert.

It was later that night that the trouble started.

Mike always enjoyed a last game, or two or three, before going to sleep. He was struggling to reach the final level of Jungle Quest, a particularly tricky new platform game, when the jungle and the gorillas and the tigers disappeared and the screen went blank.

Letters appeared across the screen:

HELP ME.

Then more letters:

I'M INNOCENT.

A picture appeared on the screen. It was a nightmarish cartoon, full of twisted and distorted shapes. It showed a squat, ugly figure taking a bag from a safe, running outside, emptying the bag's contents into a tin, and carrying the tin into a little garden, where three bushes grew under a wall. The figure buried the tin under the middle bush. Then it took the empty bag back inside, and put it into a knapsack.

A tall skinny figure appeared, opened the knapsack and found the bag. More cartoon figures appeared, and grabbed the tall one.

The screen went blank.

Mike stared uneasily at the screen. There had been nothing funny about the cartoon. Somehow it filled him with a sense of horror. What could possibly be causing it? A fault in the game? A new computer virus?

He loaded another game, a space shoot-'em-up called Starfighter. Halfway through the game the warring spaceships vanished, the same messages appeared and the same cartoon played itself out.

Mike tried a road-race game called Death Warriors, and a treasure quest game, Castle Doom.

Same result every time – the messages and the cartoon. Same strange sensations of horror and despair.

Filled with uneasy fears, Mike gave up and went to

bed. He slept badly, haunted by nightmares in which a great red shape roared down on him.

On Sunday afternoon, Mike's best friend, Chuck, came round with some games of his own. They played them through on the computer – no problems at all.

But that night, when Mike was playing alone, it all happened again. The messages:

HELP ME, I'M INNOCENT.

The cartoon of the robbery. This time, after the cartoon, there was another message:

PLEASE HELP ME. I DEPEND ON YOU.

A sense of despair seemed to rise out of the computer like a black cloud.

That night Mike had nightmares again. Something huge and red was roaring down to crush him . . .

At breaktime on Monday, Mike went to see his teacher, Miss Phelps. He told her about buying the computer and described the woman on the stall.

Miss Phelps frowned. 'That would be Mrs Harris. What about her?'

'Could you tell me her address? I need to ask her something about the computer.'

Mike went round that afternoon, straight after school.

Mrs Harris recognized him at once. 'Is it about the computer? I hope it hasn't broken down. I don't really understand them.'

'Not exactly broken down,' said Mike. 'But there's something very strange about that computer. The person who owned it before me . . .'

'My son, Peter.'

'Did something happen to him?'

The woman stared at him. 'You mean you don't know?'

'No, honestly.'

'You'd better come inside.'

In her little kitchen, Mrs Harris told Mike the whole story.

'Peter was a year above you at school – I don't suppose you'd have known him. Some money was stolen from the Head's office. Money that had been taken out of the bank to pay for a school trip abroad. There was a search and they found the cloth bank bag in Peter's bag – and everyone knew we were hard-up since my husband died.' She sighed. 'Peter swore he hadn't touched the money, and the Head sent him home "to think things over". She said the police would be called next day if the money wasn't returned. Peter set off home on his bike. It was raining and he must have been worried and upset. The bike skidded and went under a bus . . . he was killed at once.'

'I'm sorry,' said Mike. 'I heard about the accident. I didn't realize that was your son.'

Mrs Harris was trying not to cry. 'The Head came round to see me afterwards. She was really upset. She said nothing more would be said about the money. The jumble sale on Saturday was to raise some more. So I took all Peter's things to sell, just to help.'

Mike saw a photograph of a tall, thin boy on the mantelpiece. 'Is that Peter?'

Mrs Harris nodded sadly. 'I'm sure he didn't take that money. But everyone thinks he did – and now that he's dead there's just no way to prove he didn't.'

With a shiver of fear, Mike saw that the boy in the photo was the tall figure in the cartoon. He'd been getting messages from a ghost!

Suddenly Mike realized that he knew the squat figure in the cartoon as well. He said goodbye to Mrs Harris and hurried back to school. He felt frightened and determined at the same time. Things couldn't go on like this. Something had to be done – and he was the only one to do it. The ghost in the computer was depending on him!

As Mike went through the main door, old Sam, the

caretaker, stuck his head out of his little cubbyhole. He was a short, thickset, nasty old man, hated by staff and pupils alike.

'Whaddayouwant?' he growled.

'Left my maths book in the classroom,' gabbled Mike. 'Need it for homework.' He hurried past, feeling old Sam's suspicious eyes on his back. Making his way through the empty echoing corridors, he went right through the school, out of the back entrance and into the playground. There was a locked gate in the playground fence and Mike climbed over it, landing in the little garden behind the caretaker's house. There were three rosebushes against the wall, just as in the cartoon. Mike grabbed a spade leaning against the wall, went to the middle bush and started digging frantically.

The hole grew deeper and deeper and Mike started wondering if he'd made a terrible mistake. Then the spade chinked on something metallic – and a shadow fell over him.

Mike looked up. It was old Sam, his face twisted with rage. He snatched the spade from Mike's hand and raised it high . . .

A shrill whistle rang out and old Sam froze like someone in a game of statues.

Mike looked up and saw a burly figure in a tracksuit vaulting the fence. It was Mr Miller the PE master, the inevitable referee's whistle round his neck. 'What's going on?' he roared.

Mike dropped to his knees and scrabbled in the soft earth at the bottom of the hole, coming up with a big round tin.

'I saw Sam burying this soon after that money was stolen,' he said quickly. He handed the tin to Mr Miller, who wrenched off the lid. The tin was stuffed with bank-notes.

Mr Miller snatched the spade away from old Sam and took him firmly by the arm. 'The Head's still in her office. I think we'd better have a little chat.'

Old Sam denied everything, but since the police later found his house stuffed with stolen goods, it didn't do him much good. Mrs Harris received a full apology, and the promise of a school memorial service for Peter.

Later that night, when all the fuss and congratulations were over, Mike loaded a game at random into the computer.

He wasn't a bit surprised when, instead of the game, a cartoon appeared on the screen.

It showed a little figure that Mike recognized as himself digging under a rosebush and finding a tin.

A squat figure crept up on him, snatched the spade and threatened him.

A burly figure bounded over the fence and grabbed the squat one, leading him away.

All three figures vanished, and a tall, skinny figure appeared, hands clenched above its head in triumph. Letters appeared underneath it:

THANKS, MATE.

Then more letters:

GOODBYE!

Figure and letters faded away. The ghost was gone.

'Goodbye, Peter,' said Mike. 'Glad I could help.' And with a sigh of relief, he switched off the computer and went to bed.

Barker

Peter Dickinson

There was a rich old woman called Mrs Barker who lived in a pokey little house at the top of a street so steep that it had steps instead of pavements. Mrs Barker could look all the way down the street from her windows and watch people puffing up the steps to bring her presents. Quite a lot of people did that, because Mrs Barker didn't have any sons or daughters or nieces or nephews, only what she called 'sort-ofs'. Sort-of-nieces, sort-of-nephews, sort-of-cousins and so on.

You want an example? Mr Cyril Blounder's mother's father's father's mother's sister had married

Mrs Barker's father's mother's brother. That made Mr Blounder a very sort-of sort-of, but it didn't stop him bringing Mrs Barker lettuces from his garden and hoping that one day she'd die and leave him some money in her will. When he came Mrs Barker's maid, Hannah, would bring him camomile tea, which he pretended to like, while Mrs Barker looked in the lettuces for slugs.

Most of the other sort-ofs did much the same, and they always got given camomile tea, and they all pretended to like it, because of the will. When they left, Mrs Barker would stand at her window and watch them go muttering down the hill. *She* knew what they were thinking.

Whenever a new sort-of was born Mrs Barker always sent a silver napkin-ring for a christening present, with a name on it. She chose the name herself, without asking the parents, so that was what the child got called. The parents usually decided it was worth it, because of the will. Mrs Barker preferred what she called 'sensible names'. She wrote them down in the back of her notebook to make sure she didn't choose the same one twice.

After that Mrs Barker paid no attention to the child until it was eight years old. Then she used to send a message inviting it to tea. So the parents would dress the child in its smartest clothes and take it up the steps, reminding it several times on the way to say 'Please' and 'Thank you' and not to make faces when it drank the camomile tea. (Some parents used to give their children camomile tea for a week before the visit, for practice.)

But more important than any of that advice was that when Mrs Barker asked the child what it wanted for a present it must choose something *really worth having*.

Because whatever it wanted, it got.

It was very extraordinary. Mrs Barker wasn't at all generous in other ways. She sent the most miserable mingy presents to the sort-ofs at Christmas, when they all bought her beautiful things they couldn't really afford, but just this once in their lives . . .

She would peer at each child with sharp little eyes and croak in her sour old voice, 'Well, what would you like for a present?' And the child would open its eyes as wide as it could and say a racing-bike *please* or a pony *please* or a huge model railway lay-out *please* . . . Mrs Barker would write the request down in her notebook and put it away, but when the child was gone she would take out the notebook and cross off one of the names in the back.

A few days later the present would come, and it would be the best you could buy – the bike with the most gears, the briskest little pony, the most complicated railway set. But it would be the last good present that child ever got from Mrs Barker.

All this went on for years and years, until there were sort-ofs who'd been to tea with Mrs Barker when *they* were eight, now taking their own children up the steps and telling them to say please and thank you and above all to choose a present *really worth having* . . .

One of these later sort-ofs was called Molly. (Her parents had hoped to call her Claudinetta, but it said Molly on her ring.) She was taken up the steps wearing a pink bow in her hair and a pale blue frock with a white lacy apron crackling new, and told all the usual things. Hannah opened the door for her and asked the parents to be back at half past five, and Molly went in alone.

As soon as the door was shut, Molly undid the ribbon in her hair and took off the lacy apron and put them on a chair in the hall before she went into Mrs Barker's parlour and shook hands. Mrs Barker's hand was cold and dry, with loose slithery skin. She pursed her purple lips and peered at Molly.

'You were wearing a pink bow when you came up the steps,' she said.

'I took it off,' said Molly.

Mrs Barker puffed out her cheeks like a frog, but

didn't say anything. Hannah brought in the tea, thin little sandwiches, tiny dry cakes and a steaming teapot.

'Do you like camomile tea?' she asked.

'Not much, thank you, but I'll drink it if you want me to.'

Mrs Barker puffed out her cheeks again and peered at Molly, craning her neck like an old tortoise.

'What do you drink at home?' she said.

'Milk. Or orange juice. Or just water.'

Mrs Barker tinkled a small glass bell and when Hannah came she told her to bring Molly a glass of milk. After that they ate tea. Then they played an old-fashioned card game. Then they did a jigsaw. And then Mrs Barker glanced out of the window and said, 'I can see your father coming up the steps. It is time for you to go. Would you like me to put the bow back in your hair?'

Molly ran and fetched the ribbon and apron and Mrs Barker tied them with trembling old fingers.

'Now,' she said, 'I expect you would like a present.'

Molly had been meaning to ask for a record-player, though she hadn't felt comfortable about it. Her parents had been so eager, so excited about the idea of a present *really worth having*, and now there was something strange in Mrs Barker's dry old voice, as though she was getting herself ready for a disappointment . . .

So without thinking Molly said what she'd felt all along.

'I don't think people should give each other presents till they know each other properly.'

Mrs Barker puffed out her cheeks.

'Very well,' she said.

'Thank you all the same,' said Molly. 'And thank you for the tea.'

Then her father knocked on the door and took her home.

Naturally her family wanted to know what she'd chosen for a present, and when she said nothing they didn't believe her. But nothing came and nothing came and they were furious, while all the other sort-ofs were filled with glee. (None of the sort-of families liked each other much, but that didn't stop them passing the gossip round.)

Then, several weeks later, a message came that Mrs Barker would like Molly to come to tea again, and she was not to dress up specially. This time there were hot buttered scones and fresh chocolate cake and not a whiff of camomile tea anywhere. But nothing was said about presents.

The same thing happened a few weeks later, and a few weeks later still. Now Molly's family was filled with glee and all the other sort-ofs were furious. None of their children had ever been asked to a second tea, so it was obvious Mrs Barker had decided at last who was going to get her money, and now it was too late to tell the children the trick was not to ask the old so-and-so for anything at all.

This went on till almost Christmas, when a letter came.

My dear Molly,

I believe you and I may by now be said to know each other properly, so it is time we exchanged presents. You told me on your last visit that your family dog was about to have puppies. Would you choose one for me, and I shall send you something on Christmas Day.

Yours affctntly,
Ethelswitha Barker

The family dog was a mongrel, and nobody could guess who the father of her last litter might be. Molly's parents wanted to sneak off and buy a beautiful pedigree pup and pretend it came from the litter, but Molly said Mrs Barker was much too sharp not to spot that. She chose a black-and-white male and took it up the hill to show Mrs Barker, who said Molly was to take it home and look after it till it was house-trained. She added that it was to be called Barker. (A sure sign, most of the sort-ofs thought, that she was losing her wits. Naming a dog after your dead husband – honestly!)

Molly's Christmas present turned out to be a yellow waterproof hat and coat and a pair of blue wellies – for taking Barker for walks in wet weather, the note that came with them said.

When he was house-trained Barker went to live with Mrs Barker, and Molly would go most days to take him for a walk. Sometimes she stayed for tea, sometimes not. Time passed. More sort-ofs climbed the hill for their first tea. If they asked for presents they got them, and if they didn't Mrs Barker sent a cheque and note telling the parents to buy something the child needed.

Then people noticed that the writing on the notes was getting shaky. Next they saw the doctor going up the steps to the pokey little house three times in one week. Then an ambulance came. Soon after that Mrs Barker died. All this while Molly took Barker for walks, as usual.

All the sort-ofs were invited to hear the will read. They came, grinding their teeth, except for Molly's parents, who did their best not to look too triumphant, though they'd already decided on the grand house outside the town which Molly was going to buy with her money. It had a lovely big garden for her to run about in.

By the time the lawyer had finished reading the will *everybody* was grinding their teeth.

Mrs Barker had left some money to Hannah, enough for her to retire and be comfortable. That wasn't too bad. But then she had left the rest, the whole lot, an enormous amount, to Barker!

And they weren't even going to get their hands on it when Barker died. After that it was going to charity. Until then it was all Barker's. Molly was to be Barker's guardian. There was a lot of legal language, with trustees and heaven knows what, but what it all meant was that Molly was the only person who knew what Barker wanted. If she said Barker was to have something, he was to get it. If not, the money stayed in the bank. And provided Barker lived till Molly was sixteen, she was the one who was going to choose the charities which got the money in the end.

Some of the sort-ofs talked about going to law to have the will altered, but the lawyers said it was all very carefully drawn up and in any case no one could be sure who would get the money if they did get the will changed – it would probably have gone straight to the charities. So they decided to put up with it.

Almost at once Molly's parents realized this mightn't be too bad, after all. Barker needed a big garden to run about in, didn't he, and it happened there was this suitable house outside the town . . .

Molly said she'd go and see what Barker thought (though really she spent most of the time talking to Hannah). When she came back she said Barker wanted to stay in his own home, with Hannah to look after him, and Hannah didn't mind. (It was her home too – she'd lived there since she was sixteen.)

Molly's parents were *not* pleased and there was a real row, but Molly stuck to her guns. She kept saying Barker had made up his mind. Her father stormed off to the lawyers next morning, but they said the same thing. It was absolutely clear. If Molly said Barker wanted to stay in his own house, that was that. You may think it was tough-minded of Molly to stick it out, but she was a tough-minded girl. Perhaps that was why Mrs Barker had chosen her.

And she had something to help her. On the day the will had been read, one of the lawyers had given her a letter and told her she wasn't to show it to anyone else. He hadn't even read it himself. It said:

My dear Molly,

You will now know the contents of my will. It is no doubt very selfish of me to amuse myself in this manner, but I am a selfish old person and that's that. When I was young I inherited a ridiculous amount of money, but it was all tied up in Trusts until I was twenty-five, so I got no fun out of it when I was a child. I have always resented this.

I see no reason why any of my connections should inherit my money. It will do far more good if it goes to charity, but it amuses me to think that before that a child might have some fun spending a little of it, as I never did. That is why I devised a little test to choose a child who was likely to be level-headed about money. I am glad it was you who passed the test.

If I were to leave the money to you till you are of age, people would insist on it being spent 'for your own good', and you would have very little say in the matter. That is why I have left it to Barker. My will says you are to be his guardian, but really it is the other way about. He is there to protect you – you are quite clever enough to see how useful he will be in this role. I strongly advise you to establish the point at the earliest possible moment.

Barker is an earnest soul (as I am not), and I think he will make a very good guardian.

Yours affctntly,
Ethelswitha Barker

So Molly did what the letter suggested and 'established the point'. She liked their own home, and so did her parents, really. The other one was much too grand for them, and after a few weeks her parents began to think so too.

But soon the other sort-ofs realized that Molly's

family weren't the only ones who could suggest things Barker might like. They would stop Molly while she was taking him for one of his walks and say he looked a bit off-colour, and wouldn't a bit of sea-air do him good? Now it happened there was this holiday villa in Cornwall, a real snip, though he wouldn't want to use it all the time, would he, and maybe when he wasn't there it would be best if one of the Frossetts (or the McSniggs, or the Blounders, or the Globotzikoffs, or whichever of the sort-of families had thought of the scheme), went and took care of the place. For a suitable fee, perhaps.

Molly said Barker would think it over. The following week, she explained Barker thought he'd like to go on a rabbiting holiday this year, with Molly, of course, but he didn't want her to be lonely so she'd better bring a few friends and her mum and dad to drive him about to good rabbiting places. Barker paid for the petrol and the hotel rooms.

A bit later a new baby sort-of was born and had to be christened. Barker sent a silver napkin-ring, but without a name on it. Privately Molly wondered what would have happened if she'd told the silversmith to put 'Bonzo', but she explained that Barker didn't think it was quite right for a dog to tell people what to call their children.

And then one day in the supermarket Molly heard

two mothers of sort-of families chatting about the old days, and the excitement of taking their children up to have tea with Mrs Barker, and thinking of *really worthwhile* presents, and wondering whether by any chance little Sam or Betsy would be the one . . .

Molly talked to Barker about it on their next walk, and the upshot was that the notes started coming again, inviting the children to tea when it was their turn. It was a bit different, because Barker didn't ask questions the way Mrs Barker used to, and the food was better, and there was Molly to talk to and play with, but there was always camomile tea (or that's what Molly said it was, though it didn't taste much different from ordinary tea).

In fact, it all became rather like an old custom, which people have forgotten the reason for, but go on doing because they've always done it and it's a bit picturesque and so on. And there were the presents, of course. They were as good as ever, but somehow it didn't seem quite so mean and grabby asking for them, which is what people in their heart of hearts had probably felt, just as Molly had. And nobody now thought that Barker was going to leave all his money to a child who said 'Please' and 'Thank you' properly or an adult who turned up on the doorstep with a particularly nice present.

Mr Cyril Blounder, quite early on, did climb the steps one day with a bone he swore he'd dug up in his allotment, though it looked remarkably fresh. Hannah gave him camomile tea on the doorstep, and all the other sort-ofs felt he'd made a fool of himself and nobody else tried it.

Time passed. Nothing much new happened. Molly got older, and so did Barker. You'd have thought he was rather a dull dog if you met him, but he had interesting ideas. He longed to travel, Molly said, but he couldn't because of the quarantine, so instead he used to send Hannah and her sister who lived somewhere up in the North on annual holidays to exciting places, and Hannah would come back and show him her slides. He gave generously to charities on flag-days – not only to the RSPCA – and took a keen interest in nature preservation. He had some handsome trees planted in the park, with a bench under them which said:

IN FOND MEMORY OF ETHELSWITHA
BARKER
Loving Mistress

Strangers didn't know quite what to make of that, but none of the local people thought it odd.

In fact, one year there was a proposal to have

Barker elected Mayor. It was only half-serious, of course, but it worried the real parties enough to pay lawyers to find out whether you can elect a dog mayor, which you can't. But he might have got in. For a dull dog, he was surprisingly popular.

One lucky result from Barker's point of view was that he got quite an active love-life. In a town like that, most people had pedigree dogs and used to send the bitches off to be mated. They tried to shoo mongrels away when their bitches were on heat, but it almost became a sort of status symbol to let your bitch have one litter of Barker's pups, so after a few years there were quite a lot of his children in the town – Barker's own sort-ofs. They weren't sort-ofs because their relationship with him was complicated, like Mrs Barker's had been. He was their father and they were his children. That was usually clear from the black-and-white patches. They were sort-of collies and sort-of labradors and sort-of dachshunds and so on.

Curiously, people didn't mind having these mongrels born to their prize bitches, and even more curiously this wasn't because Barker was so rich – he didn't send the family a huge present when it happened, only the right number of collars, with names for the puppies on them. It was because the whole town was proud of having him around. He was odd, and different, and when nothing much was happening in the world, reporters would come and write stories for their newspapers about him.

Of course they never got it quite right – reporters don't. It was difficult for them to understand the difference it made, all that money belonging to a dog, and not a person. When old Mrs Barker had been alive people used to think about her money a lot, envying her or scheming how to wheedle cash out of her, or complaining about her not spending it on things they thought important. But somehow when the money belonged to a dog it stopped being so serious. There were still schemes and complaints, of course (you don't change people *that* much), but whoever was listening to the schemer or complainer was always likely to switch the conversation into jokes about Barker, almost as though the money wasn't real. It was, of course – it got trees planted and the spire repaired and it endowed nature trails and sent the over-sixties on coach trips and bought a site for the Youth Club – but it didn't *matter* the way it had seemed to before. Even the sort-of families stopped being as spiteful about each other as they used to be – the money was out of everyone's reach now, so there wasn't much point.

Dogs don't live as long as humans, so it wasn't long before people started to fuss about Barker's health, and knit coats for him to wear in the winter – though he had a perfectly good thick coat of his own – and speak sharply to deliverymen who hurtled round corners in their vans. Barker was a fool about traffic. Of course Hannah was supposed to keep him locked in and Molly always fastened his lead when they were walking anywhere near roads, but if he saw a cat or smelt a rabbit there was absolutely no holding him, or he'd manage to slip out on one of his love-affairs while Hannah had the door open to take in the milk. The Town Council had notices put up at the most dangerous places, saying CAUTION: DOG CROSSING, but they weren't much use as Barker never crossed twice in the same place.

Still, he bore a charmed life for eight years. He had lots of narrow escapes. Strangers driving through sometimes hit lamp posts or traffic islands trying to avoid him, and they couldn't understand why everybody was furious with *them*, and why there were always a dozen witnesses ready to come forward saying it was *their* fault.

The over-sixties coach got him in the end – coming back from a trip Barker had paid for himself. Molly said that Barker had always wanted a really good send-off, so there was a jolly funeral with masses to eat and drink for the whole town, and a fun-fair and fireworks.

After that Molly spent a whole week with the lawyers, organizing which charities should get Barker's money. Practically all of it went to ordinary sensible places, a bit to the RSPCA of course, but mostly things like Cancer Research and War on Want. But Molly kept one per cent aside (that doesn't sound very much, but Mrs Barker really had been enormously rich, so it was still a useful amount) for a special charity she had set up. The lawyers had had a lot of trouble making it legal, but she'd insisted it was what Barker wanted, so they managed it somehow.

That was why all the families in the town which had one of Barker's puppies as their pet got a surprise cheque through the letter box, with a letter saying it was to be spent exclusively for the benefit of their dog, and the youngest person in the house was the only one who could say what that dog wanted.

It was an idea that would have amused Mrs Barker, Molly thought, and made her wrinkle her lips into her sour little smile – sort-ofs getting something in the end. Only not her sort-ofs. Barker's.

Nothing To Be Afraid Of

Jan Mark

'Robin won't give you any trouble,' said Auntie Lynn. 'He's very quiet.'

Anthea knew how quiet Robin was. At present he was sitting under the table and, until Auntie Lynn mentioned his name, she had forgotten that he was there.

Auntie Lynn put a carrier bag on the armchair.

'There's plenty of clothes, so you won't need to do any washing, and there's a spare pair of pyjamas in case – well, you know. In case . . .'

'Yes,' said Mum firmly. 'He'll be all right. I'll ring you tonight and let you know how he's getting along.'

She looked at the clock. 'Now, hadn't *you* better be getting along?'

She saw Auntie Lynn to the front door and Anthea heard them saying goodbye to each other. Mum almost told Auntie Lynn to stop worrying and have a good time, which would have been a mistake because Auntie Lynn was going up North to a funeral.

Auntie Lynn was not really an aunt, but she had once been at school with Anthea's mum, and she was the kind of person who couldn't manage without a handle to her name; so Robin was not Anthea's cousin. Robin was not anything much, except four years old, and he looked a lot younger; probably because nothing ever happened to him. Auntie Lynn kept no pets that might give Robin germs, and never bought him toys that had sharp corners to dent him or wheels that could be swallowed. He wore balaclava helmets and bobble hats in winter to protect his tender ears, and a knitted vest under his shirt in summer in case he overheated himself and caught a chill from his own sweat.

'Perspiration,' said Auntie Lynn.

His face was as pale and flat as a saucer of milk, and his eyes floated in it like drops of cod-liver oil. This was not so surprising as he was full to the back teeth with cod-liver oil; also with extract of malt, concentrated orange juice and calves-foot jelly. When you picked him up you expected him to squelch, like a hot-water bottle full of half-set custard.

Anthea lifted the tablecloth and looked at him.

'Hello, Robin.'

Robin stared at her with his flat eyes and went back to sucking his woolly doggy that had flat eyes also, of sewn-on felt, because glass ones might find their way into Robin's appendix and cause damage. Anthea wondered how long it would be before he noticed that his mother had gone. Probably he wouldn't, any more than he would notice when she came back.

Mum closed the front door and joined Anthea in looking under the table at Robin. Robin's mouth turned down at the corners, and Anthea hoped he would cry so that they could cuddle him. It seemed impolite to cuddle him before he needed it. Anthea was afraid to go any closer.

'What a little troll,' said Mum sadly, lowering the tablecloth. 'I suppose he'll come out when he's hungry.'

Anthea doubted it.

Robin didn't want any lunch or any tea.

'Do you think he's pining?' said Mum. Anthea did not. Anthea had a nasty suspicion that he was like this all the time. He went to bed without making a fuss and fell asleep before the light was out, as if he were too bored to stay awake. Anthea left her bedroom door open, hoping that he would have a nightmare so that she could go in and comfort him, but Robin slept all night without a squeak, and woke in the morning as flat-faced as before. Wall-eyed Doggy looked more excitable than Robin did.

'If only we had a proper garden,' said Mum, as Robin went under the table again, leaving his breakfast eggs scattered round the plate. 'He might run about.'

Anthea thought that this was unlikely, and in any case they didn't have a proper garden, only a yard at the back and a stony strip in front, without a fence.

'Can I take him to the park?' said Anthea.

Mum looked doubtful. 'Do you think he wants to go?'

'No,' said Anthea, peering under the tablecloth. 'I don't think he wants to do anything, but he can't sit there all day.'

'I bet he can,' said Mum. 'Still, I don't think he should. All right, take him to the park, but keep quiet about it. I don't suppose Lynn thinks you're safe in traffic.'

'He might tell her.'

'Can he talk?'

Robin, still clutching wall-eyed Doggy, plodded beside her all the way to the park, without once trying to jam his head between the library railings or get run over by a bus.

'Hold my hand, Robin,' Anthea said as they left the house, and he clung to her like a lamprey.

The park was not really a park at all; it was a garden. It did not even pretend to be a park and the notice by the gate said KING STREET GARDENS, in case anyone tried to use it as a park. The grass was as green and as flat as the front-room carpet, but the front-room carpet had a path worn across it from the door to the fireplace, and here there were more notices that said KEEP OFF THE GRASS, so that the gritty white paths went obediently round the edge, under the orderly trees that stood in a row like the queue outside a fish shop. There were bushes in each corner and one shelter with a bench in it. Here and there brown holes in the grass, full of raked earth, waited for next year's flowers, but there were no flowers now, and the bench had been taken out of the shelter because the shelter was supposed to be a summer-house, and you couldn't have people using a summer-house in winter.

Robin stood by the gates and gaped, with Doggy depending limply from his mouth where he held it by one ear, between his teeth. Anthea decided that if they met anyone she knew, she would explain that Robin was only two, but very big for his age.

'Do you want to run, Robin?'

Robin shook his head.

'There's nothing to be afraid of. You can go all the way round, if you like, but you mustn't walk on the grass or pick things.'

Robin nodded. It was the kind of place that he understood.

Anthea sighed. 'Well, let's walk round then.'

They set off. At each corner, where the bushes were, the path diverged. One part went in front of the bushes, one part round the back of them. On the first circuit Robin stumped glumly beside Anthea in front of the bushes. The second time round she felt a very faint tug at her hand. Robin wanted to go his own way.

This called for a celebration. Robin could think. Anthea crouched down on the path until they were at the same level.

'You want to walk round the back of the bushes, Robin?'

'Yiss,' said Robin.

Robin could *talk*.

'All right, but listen.' She lowered her voice to a whisper. 'You must be very careful. That path is called Leopard Walk. Do you know what a leopard is?'

'Yiss.'

'There are two leopards down there. They live in

the bushes. One is a good leopard and the other's a bad leopard. The good leopard has black spots. The bad leopard has red spots. If you see the bad leopard you must say, "Die leopard die or I'll kick you in the eye," and run like anything. Do you understand?'

Robin tugged again.

'Oh no,' said Anthea. 'I'm going *this* way. If you want to go down Leopard Walk, you'll have to go on your own. I'll meet you at the other end. Remember, if it's got red spots, run like mad.'

Robin trotted away. The bushes were just high enough to hide him, but Anthea could see the bobble on his hat doddering along. Suddenly the bobble gathered speed and Anthea had to run to reach the end of the bushes first.

'Did you see the bad leopard?'

'No,' said Robin, but he didn't look too sure.

'Why were you running, then?'

'I just wanted to.'

'You've dropped Doggy,' said Anthea. Doggy lay on the path with his legs in the air, halfway down Leopard Walk.

'You get him,' said Robin.

'No, *you* get him,' said Anthea. 'I'll wait here.' Robin moved off reluctantly. She waited until he had recovered Doggy and then shouted, 'I can see the bad leopard in the bushes!' Robin raced back to safety.

'Did you say, "Die leopard die or I'll kick you in the eye"?' Anthea demanded.

'No,' Robin said guiltily.

'Then he'll *kill* us,' said Anthea. 'Come on, run. We've got to get to that tree. He can't hurt us once we're under that tree.'

They stopped running under the twisted boughs of a weeping ash. 'This is a python tree,' said Anthea. 'Look, you can see the python wound round the trunk.'

'What's a python?' said Robin, backing off.

'Oh, it's just a great big snake that squeezes people to death,' said Anthea. 'A python could easily eat a leopard. That's why leopards won't walk under this tree, you see, Robin.'

Robin looked up. 'Could it eat us?'

'Yes, but it won't if we walk on our heels.' They walked on their heels to the next corner.

'Are there leopards down there?'

'No, but we must never go down there anyway. That's Poison Alley. All the trees are poisonous. They drip poison. If one bit of poison fell on your head, you'd die.'

'I've got my hat on,' said Robin, touching the bobble to make sure.

'It would burn right through your hat,' Anthea assured him. 'Right into your brains. *Fzzzzzzz.*'

They by-passed Poison Alley and walked on over the manhole cover that clanked.

'What's that?'

'That's the Fever Pit. If anyone lifts that manhole cover, they get a terrible disease. There's this terrible disease down there, Robin, and if the lid comes off, the disease will get out and people will die. I should think there's enough disease down there to kill everybody in this town. It's ever so loose, look.'

'Don't lift it! Don't lift it!' Robin screamed, and ran to the shelter for safety.

'Don't go in there,' yelled Anthea. 'That's where the Greasy Witch lives.' Robin bounced out of the shelter as though he were on elastic.

'Where's the Greasy Witch?'

'Oh, you can't see her,' said Anthea, 'but you can tell where she is because she smells so horrible. I think she must be somewhere about. Can't you smell her now?'

Robin sniffed the air and clasped Doggy more tightly.

'And she leaves oily marks wherever she goes. Look, you can see them on the wall.'

Robin looked at the wall. Someone had been very busy, if not the Greasy Witch. Anthea was glad on the whole that Robin could not read.

'The smell's getting worse, isn't it, Robin? I think

we'd better go down here and then she won't find us.'

'She'll see us.'

'No, she won't. She can't see with her eyes because they're full of grease. She sees with her ears, but I expect they're all waxy. She's a filthy old witch, really.'

They slipped down a secret-looking path that went round the back of the shelter.

'Is the Greasy Witch down here?' said Robin, fearfully.

'I don't know,' said Anthea. 'Let's investigate.' They tiptoed round the side of the shelter. The path was damp and slippery. 'Filthy old witch. She's certainly *been* here,' said Anthea. 'I think she's gone now. I'll just have a look.'

She craned her neck round the corner of the shelter. There was a sort of glade in the bushes, and in the middle was a stand-pipe, with a tap on top. The pipe was lagged with canvas, like a scaly skin.

'Frightful Corner,' said Anthea. Robin put his cautious head round the edge of the shelter.

'What's that?'

Anthea wondered if it could be a dragon, up on the tip of its tail and ready to strike, but on the other side of the bushes was the brick back wall of the King Street Public Conveniences, and at that moment she heard the unmistakable sound of a cistern flushing.

'It's a Lavatory Demon,' she said. 'Quick! We've got to get away before the water stops, or he'll have us.'

They ran all the way to the gates, where they could see the church clock, and it was almost time for lunch.

Auntie Lynn fetched Robin home next morning, and three days later she was back again, striding up the path like a warrior queen going into battle, with Robin dangling from her hand, and Doggy dangling from Robin's hand.

Mum took her into the front room, closing the door. Anthea sat on the stairs and listened. Auntie Lynn was in full throat and furious, so it was easy enough to hear what she had to say.

'I want a word with that young lady,' said Auntie Lynn. 'And I want to know what she's been telling him.' Her voice dropped, and Anthea could hear only certain fateful words: 'Leopards . . . poison trees . . . snakes . . . diseases!'

Mum said something very quietly that Anthea did not hear, and then Auntie Lynn turned up the volume once more.

'Won't go to bed unless I leave the door open . . . wants the light on . . . up and down to him all night . . . won't go to the bathroom on his own. He says the – the –' she hesitated, 'the *toilet* demons will get him.

He nearly broke his neck running downstairs this morning.'

Mum spoke again, but Auntie Lynn cut in like a band-saw.

'Frightened out of his wits! He follows me everywhere.'

The door opened slightly, and Anthea got ready to bolt, but it was Robin who came out, with his thumb in his mouth and circles round his eyes. Under his arm was soggy Doggy, ears chewed to nervous rags.

Robin looked up at Anthea through the bannisters.

'Let's go to the park,' he said.

Maelstrom

THERESA BRESLIN

Calum lay stretched out and quiet in his hiding place, and it was his stomach pressed flat against the rough planks which first felt the boat dip as the tide pulled her. There was a strong swell running, from the north-west he reckoned, and he could feel her steady herself to take the first high waves and then move confidently forward in the water. The chug, chug, chug of the engine changed to a deeper throb, in tune with his heartbeats. Then Calum knew that the *Rose of Sharon* had cleared the breakwater and was now heading out to open sea.

He had done it! He raised his head cautiously,

brought his knees round sideways and rolled out from underneath the locker in the lower cabin. He could hear the men talking above him. They'd be discussing the best fishing ground to head for, looking up the compass and setting their course. Calum stood up. Better to wait a little while before going on deck. He wanted them to be so far out that there would be no question of turning back when they knew he was on board.

How angry would his uncle be? He remembered the conversation he had overheard weeks ago. His mother speaking softly to Fintry in their kitchen. He was due to sail on the morning tide and Calum had begged to go.

'If I let the boy go with ye,' she had said to her brother-in-law, 'you'd see he came back safe again?'

He had heard his uncle's voice, steady in reply. 'Only the Lord knows when a boat goes out, if it'll be coming home again.' And then, 'If the sea is in him then nothing will ease him until he's a fisherman.'

There was a pause. Calum saw how his mother would be twisting her fingers nervously together.

'I'll leave it for a bit longer.'

He heard the fear in her voice. The fear that had caused his father to sell out his share in the *Rose of Sharon* and take a job ashore. He had decided that night that he would be on the next trip.

He rubbed the dirt from the porthole window and looked out. Dawn was pulling away the dark strands of night and the stars were reflected on a sequined sea. He could see the port lights shining out and the rest of the fleet around them. Ahead of them the *Neptune* and the *Mary Grace*, with the *Lady Caroline* and the *Bonny Lass* off to one side. Soon they would scatter across the face of the sea.

The cabin door opened and one of the crew came in. It was his mother's cousin, Peter.

'Calum!' He shook his head. 'Aye, Fintry always said you'd turn up one day.' He pushed the boy towards the stairs. 'You'd better go and report to the skipper. He's in the wheelhouse.'

On deck in the grey light, Calum felt the boat under his feet move with the sea. He breathed in deeply. This was where he wanted to be. He felt at once vibrantly alive and yet at peace with himself. Ahead of him, in the wheelhouse, he saw his uncle raise his head as he approached. There was no smile of welcome on his face.

'I had to do it this way,' said Calum. And his voice was not pleading. 'She would never let me go.'

'Aye,' said his uncle and he cuffed Calum gently on the head. 'Get some oilskins.' He picked up the hand-set. 'I'll get on the ship-to-shore to the coastguard station and ask them to phone down and let them know,' he said, 'afore your mother's wild with worry.'

She should have realized that he would do this eventually. Had to do it. His father would understand, Calum was sure, even though his own life had taken a different course. So different from his brother, softer and rounded where Fintry was bone and muscle. He recalled his uncle working on the boat. His strong, clever fingers coiling the heavy ropes, brown skin, tanned and toughened by sun and wind. His father's hand when he clasped it was soft. Warm, flesh-coloured and smooth to touch.

Calum spent every spare minute at the harbour with the fishermen. He was there in the mornings as they unloaded their catch, cascades of fish glittering silver among the crushed ice. He knew every lane and wynd around the port; the old cottages, painted white, pale blue, cream and green, with their red pantiled roofs. The lobster pots and orange nets stretched in front. When he was small he would watch for the *Rose of Sharon* making harbour. Then he had run to meet his uncle, and Fintry would grab him and swing him high among the masts and crying gulls, and placing Calum on his shoulder he would stride home up Shore Road.

And now he was here! Actually on board the *Rose of Sharon* and working as hard as he could to prove, as much to himself as any of the rest, that he could do it.

They winched out the nets and he struggled to keep his balance on the wet deck as he ran back and forth at the crew's bidding. This was no sailboat trip, no inshore fishing excursion set up for the summer tourists. The ache in his arms from operating the gear told him this. The sea spray stung his face and salt on his eyelids and his mouth made them sore and raw.

He took his uncle some food and a mug of tea. The radio was tuned to the weather reports. At home Calum always listened to them before falling asleep. After midnight came the close-of-day shipping forecast, a benediction in the night . . .

'Fair Isle, Fastnet and Finisterre – Shannon, Dogger, Rockall and Mallaig . . .'

His own personal evensong, and a link with the boats, far out in the fishing grounds trying to reap their harvest from the sea.

'Attention all shipping. Attention all shipping. The Met Office has issued the following gale warning.'

Fintry put down his half-eaten sandwich, leaned over and turned up the sound.

'. . . three hundred and fifty miles west. Veering west, north-west, wintry showers, storm ten, severe gale nine. Imminent.'

His uncle frowned. 'What d'ye say? Ride it out, or run for home?' Before Calum could answer, the older crewman put his head into the wheelhouse.

'Fintry.' He nodded to the horizon. 'There's a sky building up that I don't like the look of at all.'

'Aye, it's on the wireless. Draw the nets and we'll shelter in for a bit.'

The storm came in quickly, as it often did in those waters. The sky darkened as grey and blue-black cloud came between them and the sun, the wind immediately gusting and alive with malice. The sea rose and became an enemy to be fought, the implacable foe of the deep-sea fisherman.

The boat pitched suddenly as the sea took fretful hold of it and tried to wrench it away from the control of the puny mortal at the wheel. The men acted quickly, moving around Calum, and suddenly he was afraid, very afraid. Yet wasn't this partly why he had come? The danger, the thrill of trying to master the elements?

Andrew, the younger crewman, on his way aft, laughed at the boy's white face. He thumped him on the back.

'I've been in worse,' he said, 'much worse. And that was only on the Millport Ferry.'

The storm rolled and crashed, and now they were in the middle of it. There was a fork of lightning and then blinding, sheeting rain and hail drenched them in moments. The black mast stabbed its finger high, as lightning livid in the dark sky threw it into relief.

A monochrome picture seared for ever on Calum's eye.

The boat climbed into a wave. The deck lifted and Calum grabbed for a rail as he lost balance. Higher yet. Now he was almost parallel with the side. Surely they must overturn?

He heard someone laugh, right out loud, and then start to sing.

'Oh, God, our help in ages past . . .' sang Peter. He sounded confident, glorious and unafraid. Calum felt his heart lift. He relaxed his body and went with the movement of the boat as Fintry held her steady and they made headway.

Into the next wave, up and up and up. The world hesitated, trembled, and then they started down again.

Then disaster struck!

Like something from the gates of hell, a lightning ball, intense and terrible, spiralled down from the heavens and struck the mast. It was felled like a rotten tree, crashed past the wheelhouse and down into the hold. The ship's lights, the crackling radio, the singing, all failed into a deadly silence.

For several seconds Calum thought he was the only person alive – on the boat, in the universe. He was aware of a wailing like the keening of some strange animal, and as he put his hands to his mouth to stop his teeth chattering he knew that the sound was coming from him. In utter shock, he moved with great difficulty. He called out. No answer. He tried to make his way forward. But the storm had realized that this boat was now its plaything and threw it carelessly about like a child in a tantrum. He struggled forward and, wriggling under the mast, found himself with his face close to Peter's. He was caught underneath it, his arm crushed and legs twisted horribly. Calum felt the man's death-white face. It was clammy to touch. Then Peter gave a soft moan. He was alive!

Suddenly his uncle was beside him. He ran his hands across Peter's face and body.

'I'll see to him and check on Andrew. You go to the wheelhouse. The radio's down, but try a Mayday. Then take the wheel and try and hold her steady.'

Calum gaped at him, mouth open, stupid.

'DO IT!' snapped Fintry.

Calum got to his feet and staggered into the wheelhouse. The radio was dead. He hit it in anger with the flat of his hand. The wheel was spinning this way and that, as the boat was tossed by the waves and wind. He must try to steer it, he thought, else they would capsize or be swamped. But how and where?

Suddenly there was a beacon in the night, in the black, driving rain ahead of him. What was it? Two flashes, then a pause, two again.

'No,' Calum whispered.

He knew all the lighthouse signalling codes – had memorized them before he was ten years old. The ones around his shoreline he could easily recite. The Taig – two flashes every twenty seconds; the Point of Inver – one every five. And this one . . . it couldn't be. If it was the Drum then they were off course, and if so close, then in the most deadly danger.

Be calm, he ordered himself. His fingers clenched the wheel. Be precise, as his father would have been. Take care, think carefully. He looked again, staring hard into the darkness, and counted slowly. Where was it and how many? There! Now! A flash. One. Two . . . and then the count in between . . . five, six, seven. It flashed again. Twice. Oh God! It *was* the Drum.

His uncle struggled back into the wheelhouse.

'Andrew's below and unconscious. I've moved some of the weight off Peter's leg. We'll have to make harbour ourself – if we can.' He peered into the darkness. 'I'll need to get a fixing on where we are.'

Calum swallowed to stop himself stuttering.

'I think we're near the rocks at Drum.'

The light sat on the most dangerous part of their coast, perched on a large group of vicious, jagged rocks below high cliffs. With cross-currents in a channel that no craft could master, it was an area which fishermen completely avoided. Now they were caught in it. Cold certainty overwhelmed Calum.

His uncle stared out into the darkness, eyes searching until he saw the beacon. He grunted.

'Aye, it's the Drum all right. I should have known you'd not make a mistake.' He pulled a chart down.

Calum bent his head on the wheel. They were doomed, all of them. He and his uncle would be smashed with the boat on the rocks, while Peter, the most experienced of them all, who most likely knew exactly what was happening, lay frustrated and helpless, to be drowned like a kitten in a bag. Calum's grasp slackened and the wheel spun quickly through his fingers.

'Keep that wheel right!' his uncle yelled.

Calum gazed back at him. 'It's hopeless,' he said.

His uncle flung the chart aside and gripped Calum fiercely by his shoulders. 'It's never hopeless,' he shouted. 'Your father's been the lifeboat cox for twenty years. D'ye think he ever turned back when things were at their worst? How many folk would have drowned if he had given up? You always wanted to be a sailor. Now be one, and steer the damn boat!'

He picked up the chart. 'If we're going to strike, at least we might choose where and how. There's a point where the channel lies close to the shore, where the cliffs are not so high. Now the tide's out for another hour. If we can run her aground there, then we might come out of this . . .'

Calum and his uncle fought to get control of the boat. She was being pulled by the currents, cork-screwing violently in the maelstrom. As she was pushed nearer and closer in to the cliffs, Calum realized that sailing this way she would be driven straight on to the rocks. He saw in his mind the water flooding in as her back was broken on the reef. He understood now what his uncle had said. If they could bring her about, perhaps the damage would not be so bad. He dragged on the wheel, and she responded heavily. He moved his hands across and, bracing him-self against the frame of the wheelhouse, he hauled on the wheel as hard as he could.

'Good man!' his uncle cried. 'She's coming round!'

Calum felt the run of the current take her. Could they keep her side on and guide her past the high reef? His arms, shoulders and back were aching. Sweat streaked his face as he desperately tried to steer the boat while some demon grappled her away from him.

They almost had her straightened up when, with a great grinding, tearing crash, she struck. He was thrown to the floor and then out across the deck as the boat canted violently to one side, held fast in the teeth of the rocks.

Calum got to his feet, blood pouring from a cut on

his forehead. He was dizzy and sick and fought down nausea as he tried to assess the damage. She was holed, and badly, but, praise God, it was above the waterline. He ran back to his uncle.

'Take this.' Fintry wound a rope around Calum's waist and made it fast to the rail. 'Tell them at the station we need a helicopter to bring a line aboard, and a tug standing by to pull us off. They'll have to move fast. If the tide turns and we're still here, we'll be pounded to pieces.' He held the boy by his shoulders. 'Good luck.' Then he pulled Calum towards him and hugged him. He stepped back into the wheelhouse. 'Go,' he said.

Calum went back out on deck. They were very close in. A treacherous scramble would take him across to the shingle below. He pulled off his oilskins, hesitated and then discarded his lifejacket. It would only restrict him, and anyway . . . He regarded the raging sea only a metre or so away from him. If he fell in there, he doubted whether the lifejacket would be of any use.

He lowered himself from the raised side of the boat, slipped on the rocks and fell at once into the water. Immediately, the intense cold penetrated through to his bones. He swallowed salt water and, for a crazy moment, almost felt like laughing. There were about six different ways to perish at sea and it looked as if he was going to experience all of them. Then a great grey towering wave lifted him and threw him on to the tiny beach. He staggered to his feet, was violently sick and then sat down again quickly. He was dizzy and blinded with blood from the wound in his head. He would need to take time to think.

He thought of his father again. He did things slowly, carefully. The little wooden ships which he lovingly fashioned from wood and sold to the holiday-makers. He took time and patience with his models. He didn't make mistakes. Calum untied the rope and pulled the tail of his shirt from under his jacket and tore off some material. He wrapped a bandage firmly round his head, then he pulled off the heavy rubber sea boots. He tore more strips and wrapped them round his socks and then a piece around each hand. He rubbed himself furiously all over to warm himself. Then he stood up and walked purposefully towards the cliff path.

The wind was howling around him, anxious to pluck him away from the fragile hold he had on the scrub and gorse. He was almost on his hands and knees as he followed the track higher and higher. The sea boiled below him, and he imagined himself falling and his skull cracked open like a gull's egg on the rocks below.

At one point a bird flew out, screeching at his head,

and he had to rest until his heart stopped thumping and his legs ceased trembling. His hands and feet were cut and bruised when he finally levered himself over the top edge. The coastguard station was about two miles round the headland. Legs shaking and tears running down his face, Calum picked himself up from the rough grass and started to run.

'Hot drink. Bath. Bed,' his mother ordered after the doctor had left Calum's bedroom.

Calum tried to get up. His legs and arms were bruised and sore. His voice wavered.

'I have to see Fintry,' he said, 'and Peter and Andrew.'

'They're fine.' His father came into the room carrying a tray. 'I've spoken to the matron at the cottage hospital. They are going to be all right.'

'And –'

'The *Rose of Sharon* is safe in harbour.' His father smiled at him. 'Now rest, and we'll visit them in the morning.'

'I won't give up the sea,' said Calum as they entered the hospital the next day.

'No,' said his father, 'and you shouldn't either. It was different for me. I was following a family tradition, but my heart wasn't in it. Your mother could see that. I didn't love the sea the way Fintry does . . . the way you do.'

He held out his hands, palms up, and looked down at them. 'We each do according to how we are.'

Calum walked down the ward to his uncle's bed.

'She's safe,' he told him. 'She needs a bit of work, but the *Rose of Sharon* will put to sea again.'

'Calum's quite a hero, now,' his mother said.

'No,' said Fintry quietly. He took Calum's hands firmly in his own. 'He's a fisherman.'

Baggy Shorts

Alan MacDonald

'And there it is, the final whistle and Ditchley Rovers are through to a Wembley cup final for the first time in their history. The players are dancing around and hugging each other. The crowd (four parents and a kid in a pushchair) is going wild. Joss Porter, Ditchley's goal hero, runs towards the touch line with both arms in the air and salutes his dad. These are amazing scenes!'

I do commentaries like that in my head all the time – at school, on the bus, even underwater in the bath. But this commentary I was doing last Saturday afternoon was different. It was the real thing, I didn't have to make it up. Ditchley Rovers really had just made it through to our first ever Wembley final. And I scored one of the goals. OK, so the ball bounced in off my knee but that's how I sent their goalkeeper the wrong way. And OK, so the final wasn't at Wembley Stadium, it was at Wembley Park. They're very similar, except the pitch at Wembley Park has hardly any grass, and dips in the middle like a banana.

But that didn't matter to me. As I said to our manager the next day, 'We're in the final, that's all that counts.'

'Don't keep saying that, Joss,' said Dad. 'I'm trying to find Stanley Matthews.'

Dad was busy with his cigarette card collection. He's got boxes full of them. Cards he collected when he was a boy with colour pictures of ships, trains and wild birds. The ones I like best are his football cards. Famous players of the past with centre partings and teethy smiles.

Dad found the card he was looking for and held it up to show me.

'Stanley Matthews. The wizard of dribble. Now there was a real footballer. You never saw *him* kissing one of his team mates when he scored a goal.'

I nodded, but I wasn't really listening. All I could think about was Saturday and Ditchley Rovers v Top Valley. It was Top Valley's third cup final in a row.

Really there ought to be a rule against teams hogging the cup. It was well known Top Valley creamed off all the best players in the area. Their manager went round all the school matches scouting for new talent. Most of Ditchley Rovers couldn't even get in their school team (me included). But Dad said that wasn't the point – everyone deserves a chance. It's not the winning that counts, it's the taking part. Which was another way of saying Top Valley were going to thrash us 8–0 on Saturday.

'I think it'll be a close game,' I said to Dad.

He didn't answer. Too busy glueing Stanley Matthews into his album.

'I mean the cup final, Dad. We'll probably only win by one goal.'

'It doesn't matter whether you win, Joss, as long as you all play your best.'

'You think we'll lose then? Our own manager doesn't give us a chance.'

'I didn't say that.'

'They're going to bury us, aren't they, Dad?'

Dad sighed heavily. 'Can't you just stop thinking about Saturday for five minutes?'

But I couldn't stop thinking about it. It was the cup final. Ditchley Rovers had never played in a final before and we weren't likely to play in one again. The truth was we were dead lucky to be in the final. There was a flu bug going round and two of the teams we were supposed to play against had to pull out because they couldn't raise a side. In the semi-final our goalie, Flip, made a string of blinding saves and then I scored a late winner with my knee. Dad said that if Eric Cantona had been playing against us that day he probably would have tripped over and sprained his ankle during the warm-up.

The trouble was, now that we were in the cup final I couldn't help it. At school, on the bus, under water in the bath . . . I was working on a new commentary.

'And it's all over. Top Valley hang their heads. They can't believe it. Ditchley Rovers – who nobody gave a chance going into this game – have made an amazing comeback. Three goals in three minutes from deadly Joss Porter have turned the game on its head. And now he's being carried shoulder high by the Ditchley team as he lifts the cup to the crowd. The roar is deafening . . .'

It was all a dream, of course. Top Valley were going to slaughter us.

On Thursday we met for a practice session over at Wembley Park. Dad called us together for a team talk. He was wearing his navy tracksuit with the England 1966 badge on the pocket.

'Now we all know that Saturday is a big game for us. Our Joss has been going to bed with his kit on every night – just to make sure he doesn't miss the kick-off.'

Everyone looked in my direction and laughed. I hated it when Dad made stupid jokes about me. Sometimes I wished he wasn't our manager.

Dad went on. 'A cup final is special. There are plenty of kids who'd like to be in your boots on Saturday. But they're not. It's your chance, so make the most of it.'

I looked around. Matt, Flip, Sammy, Nasser and the rest were nodding their heads seriously. You could see they were as keyed up as I was.

We lined up for shooting practice against Flip.

'Flip me, Joss! Why don't you break me fingers or something?' he said as he stopped my shot.

The truth is Flip's not a bad goalie. If it wasn't for him we'd never have reached the final. He's not very big but he isn't afraid of anything. This evening he was in great form, flinging himself down to stop a shot and springing up again like a jack-in-the-box. Hardly anything got past him.

A cold wind blows across Wembley Park on a winter evening. A thin mist drifted over from the river. It was Nasser who noticed the tall kid behind the goal watching us.

'Hey, Joss,' he grinned. 'You seen old baggy shorts over there? Think he wants a game?'

I looked behind the goal. The tall kid was standing to one side of the posts with a ball tucked under his arm. He had a body like a runner bean. Somehow it held up a pair of shorts that came down to his knees and flapped in the wind. He wore a green roll-neck jumper. Above it his big ears stuck out like mug handles under a flat grey cap. The total effect was like a jumble sale on legs.

By now Sammy, Matt, Nasser and the others had noticed him. They started making sniggering comments.

'Clock the gear, eh?'

'Is that Arsenal's away strip?'

'No, must be Oxfam's.'

'Let's sign him on. He can be our secret weapon.'

'Yeah, he can hide the match ball in his shorts.'

Nasser said the last joke too loud because Baggy Shorts frowned and looked at the mud.

'Shut up!' I said. 'He'll hear you.'

A few minutes later I went to get a ball from behind the goal. Baggy Shorts was still standing there with the ball under his arm. The cold didn't seem to bother him. I wondered why he kept watching us.

'Hello,' I said. 'You from round here?'

He touched his cap and nodded seriously. 'Used to be.'

'What happened? Did you move away?'

'Kind of.' There was a pause. 'I'm a goalie,' he said, looking straight at me.

'Are you?'

'Yes. I'm a good goalie.'

'I bet you are. But we've already got a goalie. Flip. He's over there.'

I jerked my head in the direction of the goal. Baggy Shorts nodded again. 'I'm a good goalie,' he repeated, bouncing the ball and catching it in his big pale hands. I noticed it was made of heavy brown leather held together with a lace.

'We're playing here Saturday in the cup final,' I said. 'You can come and watch if you want.'

Baggy Shorts nodded again. 'I never played in a final. Never.' He looked away into the distance as if there was something just out of sight. The mist had got thicker. I realized I was shivering.

'Well, kick-off's at three.' I said. 'Come and support us. I gotta go now. See you.'

I ran back to the others. The shooting practice had stopped. Everyone was gathered round Flip who was sitting on the ground. Dad was kneeling beside him, looking at his nose which was an ugly swollen red.

'Ah flip me! Don't touch it!' he cried out.

'What happened?' I asked.

'I didn't know he was coming for the cross,' said Sammy. 'I was jumping to head the ball and Flip came out and somehow . . . I headed him instead.'

'It was my flippin' ball,' moaned Flip. 'I called for it.'

'Will he be all right?' I asked Dad. 'For Saturday, I mean? He will be able to play on Saturday, won't he?'

Dad helped Flip to his feet. 'It's probably just a nasty bruise. But I'll take him to the hospital to get it looked at just in case. The rest of you better go home. It's getting late.'

We trooped miserably off the field.

'Nice one, Sammy,' I said. 'If Flip can't play on Saturday there goes our only chance. Without him Top Valley will murder us.'

As we were leaving I remembered Baggy Shorts again. I turned back to wave goodbye. But he'd gone, melted away into the mist.

It was Cup Final day, and we were sitting in the dressing room in silence, all staring at the floor. Dad had just asked if anyone wanted to play in goal. The news about Flip was bad. The hospital said his nose might be broken; it was hard to tell until the swelling went down. Broken or not, there was no way he could play in a cup final.

We'd have to play our sub, Gormless Gordon, at right back. That meant someone else had to go in goal.

The news was greeted in the dressing room as if someone had died. There was no point in kidding ourselves any longer. We'd lost the final before the game started. I could hear the commentary running through my head:

'And it's another one! This time through the goal-keeper's legs. This is turning into a massacre. 32–0 to Top Valley and there's still half an hour to go! Ditchley Rovers must wish the final whistle would blow and put them out of their misery.'

That's why no one was volunteering to put on the green jersey. The goalkeeper always gets the blame. He's the one the rest of the team picks on when they're losing badly. That's why I couldn't believe it when Dad spoke to me.

'Joss, you've played in goal before.'

I looked up in horror. 'That was only messing around in the park. I've never played in a proper match.'

'There's always a first time. You could do it.'

'Dad! No way! I'm a striker. I'd be hopeless in goal.'

'Well, somebody's got to. Listen, all of you, Flip

isn't coming. We've just got to put out the best team we can. And if we lose it's no disgrace. Now I'll ask again – is anyone willing to go in goal?'

I looked around at the rest of the team. Pleading with them: *'Not me, anyone but me, somebody else do it, please.'* No one would look at me. They stared at the floorboards as if they wanted to crawl underneath.

'Right, that's it then. Joss, you're in goal first half,' said Dad, losing patience. I picked up the green jersey he threw at me. It wasn't fair. He shouldn't be manager if he was going to pick on me.

Top Valley were already out on the pitch in their smart new kit. Red and white striped shirts with their names on the back. Just like professionals.

'Come on, you Valley kings! You'll murder this lot!' shouted their manager from the touch line. Most of their team were bigger than us. I recognized Gary Spencer who is top scorer for our school team. He gave me a nod.

'Hi, Joss! They're not playing you in goal, are they?'

I nodded miserably.

'You *must* be desperate,' he said, rubbing his hands together. You could see him imagining all the goals he was going to score.

* * *

The game kicked off. Top Valley sent the ball straight down the wing. We didn't clear it. A high ball came over. I started to come out for it, then changed my mind. As I tried to get back, the ball thumped into the corner of the net. Gary Spencer wheeled away with his arms going like windmills.

'Goooooooooal!'

Nasser shook his head at me in disbelief. 'Why didn't you come out?'

'Why didn't you mark him if you're so great?' I snapped back.

The rest of the first half we defended grimly, hardly ever getting past the halfway line. Top Valley went two up after twenty minutes. After that, I made a few lucky saves and we kept the score down by keeping ten players back and booting the ball anywhere.

As the minutes ticked toward half-time, I noticed the mist drifting in again from the river. I heard a ball bounce behind me and there was Baggy Shorts. He was wearing the same as before – grey cap, green jumper, huge baggy white shorts.

'Hi,' I said. 'Come to watch us get beaten?'

He stood to one side of my goal.

'Where's your goalie?' he asked.

'Broke his nose. Couldn't come. That's why they stuck me in goal.'

He nodded thoughtfully. 'I'm a goalie,' he said.

'Yeah,' I replied, 'you told me that the other day.'

'I'm good.'

'But you don't play for our team.'

'I could do, though.'

Baggy Shorts took off his flat cap and held it in both hands. His hair was cut short over his big ears and parted in the middle. He looked at me, his eyes full of longing.

'Please. I never played in a final. Never. Give me a chance.'

It came out in a rush. Then he put his cap back on and waited.

At that moment the referee blew for half time.

'You must be bonkers, Joss,' said Sammy. 'Look at him. He turns up out of nowhere in his grandma's bloomers and you want to play him in goal.'

'But we haven't got a goalkeeper,' I argued. 'We're going to get beaten anyway. What have we got to lose?'

'Another ten goals,' said Nasser.

I pulled off the green jersey.

'Well, who's going in goal for the second half then? I've done my bit.'

Nobody took the jersey from me. We all looked at Dad. It was his decision. He stared across at Baggy

Shorts who stood a little way off, bouncing his old leather ball.

'Everyone deserves their chance,' said Dad.

Gormless Gordon went off and Baggy Shorts came on as a sub. I could see the Top Valley players grinning as Baggy Shorts took the field. He ran past them, shorts flapping in the wind and cap pulled down over his eyes.

Gary Spencer sidled up to me as we lined up for kick-off.

'Where'd you get him then? On special offer at Tesco's?'

I stared back at him coldly. I'd had enough of being the joke team. If we were going to lose then the least we could do was make a fight of it.

From the kick-off, Sammy passed to me and I burst through the middle. Top Valley were caught half asleep and my pass found Nasser in the penalty area. He shot first time, low into the corner. 2–1.

It was the start we needed to get back in the game. But it also stung Top Valley awake. They soon had the ball back up our end and Gary Spencer carved his way through our defence. He left three players on the ground as he raced into the penalty area.

There was only Baggy Shorts left between him and the goal. Spencer looked up to pick his spot. It was too easy. But in that second, Baggy Shorts came racing off his line like a greyhound and threw himself on the ball. Spencer couldn't take it in. One minute he had the ball, the next Baggy Shorts had whipped it off his boot and kicked it upfield. The small crowd watching clapped. Ditchley Rovers looked at each other in astonishment. Baggy Shorts wasn't just good, he was brilliant.

The rest of the game Top Valley tried to find a way to beat our new goalkeeper. They aimed for the corners. They rained in shots like cannonballs. They tried to dribble round him. But Baggy Shorts was a mind-reader. He seemed to know exactly where the ball was going. He leapt like a cat and pulled it out of the air. He rolled over, sprang to his feet, bounced the ball twice and sent it into orbit. With just ten minutes to go we got a goal back to level the scores at 2–2. Then, as the minutes ticked away, the disaster happened. Gary Spencer went through again and again Baggy Shorts dived at his feet. But this time Spencer was waiting for it. He went sprawling over the goalkeeper and lay in the mud holding his leg.

'Ahh, ref! Penalty!'

Anyone could see it was an obvious dive but the referee blew his whistle and pointed to the spot.

Spencer made a miraculous recovery to take the

penalty himself. He winked at Baggy Shorts with a smug grin on his face. Baggy Shorts didn't say a word, he went back on his goal-line. I walked away to the halfway line feeling sick. Three minutes to go and we were going to lose to the worst penalty ever given. But as Spencer placed the ball I couldn't help myself. I always do the commentary for penalties.

'And the crowd are hushed. Baggy Shorts crouches on his line. Spencer takes a run-up. He hits it hard, low, into the corner . . . it's . . . No! Baggy Shorts has saved it one-handed. An incredible save! Spencer has his head in his hands. Baggy Shorts gathers the ball. Sends a long kick upfield. Towards . . . ME! Help! Where is everybody?'

I just kept running towards the goal waiting for someone to tackle me. But nobody did. And as their goalkeeper came out I slipped the ball under his body. It rolled gently over the line. Goal – and this time I hadn't used my knee either.

The whistle went soon after. Ditchley Rovers had won the cup. 3–2 with a dramatic late winner from deadly Joss Porter. Just as I'd predicted all along. I was mobbed by the whole team, jumping on top of me until we were all rolling around in the mud, laughing. Dad was going round banging everybody on the back. I don't think he could quite believe it.

Then we had to line up for the cup to be presented.

Sammy said, 'Where's Baggy Shorts? He should go up first. He was man of the match.'

We looked around. But we couldn't find him. No one knew where he'd gone. I looked back to the goal-mouth where he'd saved the penalty, but there was no one there, only a fine mist drifting in from the river.

A few days after the cup final, Dad was working on his cigarette card collection again. I saw him stop with the glue in one hand and a card in the other. He was staring at something.

'What is it?' I asked. He handed me the card in his hand. It was from the football series. On the back it said:

Player number 132: Billy Mackworth. Goal-keeper. Despite his boyish looks, Mackworth was a talented goalkeeper for Spurs. He should have been the youngest player to play at Wembley in the 1947 cup final. Sadly he died in a road accident a few days before the game. He never played in a cup final.

There was no mistaking the picture. He looked older but the two big ears still stuck out like mug handles under his cap. The eyes stared gravely into the distance. It was Baggy Shorts.

The Man Who Understood Cats

ADRIAN ALINGTON

No, sir, I would never speak disrespectfully about a cat. I've seen too much. 'Deep,' little Joey Duggan used to say. 'Cats are deep creatures. People who think of them just as pretty pets are making a big mistake.' And if anyone ever knew, little Joey Duggan did.

I don't suppose you ever heard of Joey. His name wasn't very well known outside the profession. But he was a great little artist for all that. Animal impersonator. Cats were his speciality and really he was marvellous. How many years running he played the cat in *Dick Whittington* I wouldn't know, but every Christmas he was at it somewhere, and nearly always he stole the show. I know that because once I played Dame* in the same pantomime with him. He certainly stole the show that year. I'd like to tell you, if you've got a moment . . .

The pantomime was in a big provincial town. Bessie Bates was Principal Boy and she didn't like Joey one little bit. Dick Whittington's cat acted his master off the stage. Not that Joey ever tried any funny stuff. He was much too good an artist for that. It was just that when he got into his skin, Joey to all intents and purposes became a cat. You never saw anything so lifelike.

His secret was that he really knew and understood cats. He was crazy about them and they were crazy about him. He was the friend of all the cats in the world, that little man.

I was having a drink with him one day, and sure enough the pub cat came strolling along the bar to Joey. 'You see how he picks his way without touching anyone's drink,' said Joey. 'Dainty as a prima ballerina.' The cat came up to Joey and began rubbing against him, and Joey tickled him and made his own private cat noises to him, and it was for all the world like two pals talking.

*[*NB In a pantomime the Principal Boy is played by a woman and the Dame by a man.*]

Then Joey began to talk about cats in general, about how in ancient Egypt they had been worshipped, and so on. And then he got on to the what's-his-name of souls – you know what I mean, the idea that we all live lots of times in different forms. As far as I could make out, his idea was that he'd been a cat at one time or another, and that's what made his act come natural to him.

Presently someone called the cat and he jumped down off the bar. Joey watched him.

'Ah,' he said, 'if I could learn to jump like that, then I should be really good.'

As a matter of fact, Joey was quite a bit of an acrobat. He used to do a stunt at the end of the show, just before the finale. All of us principals used to come down the staircase, one at a time, to get our applause. But Joey used to come from the back of the dress circle, run round the edge of the circle on all fours, and then jump down on to the stage from one of the boxes. That always went big. Bessie tried to get the management to cut it out. But of course they wouldn't. It was one of the hits of the show.

We come now to a night towards the end of the season. A night I shall never forget as long as I live. We had a big house and plenty of laughs. I had a little scene with Joey in the first half of the show. Comedy stuff. He used to sidle up to me and rub himself against me and then roll on the floor for me to stroke his stomach. Then when we'd got all the laughs we could, I used to pretend to see a mouse. I used to jump on to a chair, holding up my skirts, while Joey chased the mouse off the stage. It always went well, but on this particular night it was a riot. Joey was terrific. He seemed inspired. No clowning – he just was a cat. Once I whispered to him through a big laugh: 'Great work, Joey.' But he didn't answer. He never let up when he was on the stage.

I didn't meet him again till the finale. I made my entrance down the staircase. Then Bessie came on and called: 'Puss, puss!' There was the usual answering miaow and Joey appeared from the back of the dress circle. He jumped on to the rim of the circle as usual, but he didn't do his run round. Instead, he jumped clean out of the circle into the stalls below. Somebody screamed. For a split second I thought there was going to be a panic but – and this is as true as I'm standing here – Joey landed in the aisle on his four paws as lightly as you please, and began to walk up towards the stage with his tail in the air.

And that wasn't the end, either. When he came to the front row of the stalls, he hesitated for a moment, gathered himself for a spring, as you see cats do, and jumped right across the orchestra pit on to the stage. It was like a big black panther jumping. I saw the conductor duck his head, looking as though he couldn't believe it. Well, when that happened, the audience went mad. I never heard such cheering. It went on long after the curtain had come down on us for the last time.

Bessie looked as sour as anything. I turned round to congratulate Joey, but Joey wasn't there. Instead, I saw the manager coming on with a face the colour of green cheese.

'What in heaven's name is going on?' he asked.

'Joey has been giving the performance of his life,' I told him.

'Joey was run over and killed on his way to the theatre,' he answered. 'They've just rung up from the hospital. Seems the dear little fool was trying to rescue a kitten that had run out into the traffic.'

No, sir, I shall never speak disrespectfully of cats. Not after knowing Joey Duggan.

Beauty and the Beast

Retold by Adèle Geras

A very long time ago, in a distant land, there lived a merchant. His wife had been dead for many years, but he had three daughters and the youngest was so lovely that everyone who saw her wondered at her beauty. Her name was Belle, and she was as good and kind a child as any man could wish for. When a storm at sea sank all but one of the merchant's ships, the family was left with very little money, and Belle was the only one of the three sisters who never complained.

'We shall have to clean the house now,' sighed the eldest. 'And cook as well, I daresay.'

'No more pretty new clothes for us,' moaned the

second sister. 'And no maid to dress our hair each morning and prepare our baths each night.'

'We are young and strong,' said Belle, 'and we shall manage perfectly well until Father's last ship comes to port.'

'You are a silly goose,' said the older girls. 'Hoping when there is so very little hope. The last ship probably went down with all the rest, taking our wealth with it.'

Spring turned to summer, and towards the end of summer came news that the merchant's last ship had indeed been saved and was now docked in the small harbour of a town not three days' ride from his house.

'I shall set out at once,' he said, 'and return within the week. Fortune has smiled on us at last, and I am in the mood to celebrate. What gifts shall I bring you, daughters, from the grand shops that I shall surely see on my journey?'

'Something that sparkles like a star,' said the eldest. 'A diamond, I think.'

'Something that glows like a small moon,' said the second daughter. 'A pearl to hang around my neck.'

Belle said nothing.

'And you, my little one,' said the merchant. 'What would delight your heart?'

'To see you safely back in this house after your travels would please me more than anything,' said

Belle. 'But if I have to choose a gift, then what I should like is one red rose.'

As soon as the merchant finished his business in the harbour, he set off for home. His saddle-bags were filled with gold coins, for he had sold everything that had been on board the last of his ships. Even after buying a diamond for one daughter and a pearl for another, there was plenty of money left.

'But,' he said to himself, 'there are no red roses anywhere in the town. I must look about me as I ride, and perhaps I shall see one growing wild.'

The merchant made his way home, lost in day-dreams of how he would spend his new-found wealth. Dusk fell and soon the poor man realized that he had strayed from the roadway and that his horse was making its way down a long avenue of black trees towards some lights that were shining in the distance.

'This must be a nobleman's country estate,' said the merchant to himself. Through tall wrought-iron gates, he saw the finest mansion he had ever laid eyes on. There was a lamp burning at every window.

Having no one else to talk to, the merchant said to his horse, 'The gentleman to whom all this belongs is at home, beyond a doubt, and a large party of guests with him, it would seem. Perhaps he will extend his hospitality to one who has strayed from his path.

Come, my friend. I will dismount and we will walk together up this handsome drive.'

The gates opened as the merchant touched them. When he reached the front door, he said to his horse, 'Wait here for a moment, while I announce myself.'

He stepped over the threshold, but there was no one there to greet him, and a thick white silence filled every corner of the vast hall.

'Is anyone here?' cried the merchant, and his own voice came back to him, echoing off the high walls.

He went outside again quickly and said to his horse, 'Come, we will find the stable, my friend, for everyone in the house seems to have disappeared. Still, it is a beautiful place. Perhaps I shall find a maid in the kitchen who will give me a morsel of food and show me a bed where I may spend the night, for we shall never find our way back to the highway in the dark.'

The stable was comfortable and clean, and the merchant fed his horse, and settled him in one of the empty stalls.

Then he returned to the house, thinking that by now someone would have appeared.

There was no one to be seen, but a delicious smell of food hung in the air. Yes, thought the merchant, that door, which was shut, is now open, and someone is serving a meal.

He walked into this new room and saw one place

laid at a long table. He saw a flagon of wine and one glass, and many china plates bearing every sort of delicacy a person could desire.

'Is there anyone here to join me in this feast?' said the merchant to the embroidered creatures looking down at him from the tapestries on the walls, but there was no reply, so he sat down at the table and ate and drank his fill.

'I think,' he said aloud, 'that I have come to an enchanted dwelling, and I shall now take this candlestick and see what lies upstairs. Perhaps a kind fairy has made a bed ready for me, and a bath as well.'

He went upstairs, and saw that there, too, the lamps had been lit, so that he had no need of his candle. He opened the first door on a long corridor and found himself in the most sumptuous of bedrooms. The sheets were made of silk, and soft towels had been laid out on the bed. He could see curls of steam drifting from an adjoining chamber, and as he pushed open the door, he discovered a bath, ready for him to step into.

'Whoever you are,' said the merchant to the velvet curtains that had been drawn across the windows, 'you are the most thoughtful of hosts. I can smell the lavender oil you have sprinkled in the bath . . . Maybe in the morning you will show yourself and I will be able to thank you properly.'

The merchant bathed and went to bed and fell into a dreamless sleep. When he woke up, the curtains had been pulled back, the sun was shining, and a tray with his breakfast upon it had been placed on a small table near the window. A fine set of clothes had been prepared for him, and he put it on and marvelled at how well it fitted. At first he could not find his own travel-stained garments, but they had been washed and dried and pressed and lay folded beside his saddle-bags, which he had left beside the front door the previous night.

'I must go home,' he thought to himself. 'However pleasant this place may be, I must return to my children. I shall fetch my horse from the stable and set off at once.'

The gardens of the mansion were a small paradise. Seeing them spread out before him reminded the merchant that he still had not found a red rose for Belle.

'In this garden,' he thought, 'there may still be red roses, even though autumn is nearly upon us. I shall pick just one, if I see some, and be gone.'

Flowers still bloomed in the garden, but the merchant had to walk along many paths before he came to a bush covered with red roses that had just blossomed. He chose the plumpest and smoothest; the most luscious and velvety of all the flowers he could see, and snapped it off the bush.

At that moment, an anguished roar filled the air and there, towering over him, was the most hideous creature the merchant had ever seen; a being from the worst of his nightmares; something that could not be human even though it stood upright and wore a man's clothes and spoke in a man's voice.

'Ungrateful wretch!' this Beast said. 'All that I have done for you: fed you and clothed you and sheltered you . . . all that is not enough. No, you must steal a bud from my most precious rosebush. There is no punishment but death for such ingratitude.'

The merchant began to weep.

'I did not mean it as theft,' he said. 'The owner of this place – you – I knew how kind you must be. I thought a rosebud was but a trifling thing after all the wonders you had lavished on me. It is a present for my youngest daughter. I promised her a red rose before I set out on my journey, or I would never have touched anything that belonged to you. I beg you, spare my life.'

'You must not judge by appearances,' said the Beast. 'I love my roses more than anything in the world, and a red rose is no trifling thing to me. Now you have plucked one for your child. I will spare your life, but only on this condition. One of your daughters must return with you in a month's time, and you must leave her here for ever. She must come of her own free will, and bear whatever fate awaits her in this place. If none of your children will make this sacrifice for you, then you yourself must return and be punished for your crime. Go now. I will wait for you and for whichever daughter may choose to accompany you.'

When the merchant reached his home, he wept as he told the story of the enchanted mansion and of what he had promised the Beast. His two elder daughters glanced first at the jewelled necklaces he had brought them and then at one another, but not a word did they utter.

Belle smiled and said, 'Dry your tears, Father. It was for the sake of my red rose that you ventured into the garden, so I shall go with you and with pleasure.'

The cold came early that autumn. As Belle and her father made their way back to the Beast's mansion, snow began to fall, and by the time they reached the wrought-iron gates, it seemed as though white sheets had been spread over the whole landscape. The merchant's heart was like a stone in his breast, and Belle was trying to cheer him as they drew near the house.

'You must not worry about me, Father, for if you do, it will make me very unhappy. I know that my happiness is your dearest wish, so for my sake, let your spirits be high. I want to remember you smiling.' Belle smiled at her father, as if to set him an example.

She said, 'This is a very handsome building, and from all that you told me about the Master of this place, he seems to be a kind and hospitable creature. I do not see anything so terrible in living here, if your life is to be spared as a consequence.'

'You have not seen the Beast,' said the merchant, shivering. 'Oh, you will change your tune when you do, my dear.'

The door opened at their touch, just as it had before.

'We have come,' the merchant called out, 'as I promised.'

His words floated up towards the ceiling, but no one appeared.

'Come,' said the merchant. 'Let us go into the banqueting hall and eat, for we have had a long journey, and you must be hungry, my dear.'

Two places had been set at the table. Belle and her father were eating with heavy hearts when the Beast came silently into the room. It was only when he spoke that Belle caught sight of him, hidden in the shadows by the door.

'Is this the daughter,' said the Beast, 'who comes here in your place?'

'Yes, I am,' Belle answered for her father. 'My name is Belle and I am happy to be in such a beautiful house, and happy to be of service to my father.'

'You will not be so happy,' said the Beast, 'once you have looked upon my face. It will fill you with horror and haunt all your dreams.'

For her father's sake, Belle knew she had to be brave. She said, 'I have heard your voice, sir, and it is as low and sweet a voice as any man ever spoke with. Your face holds no terrors for me.'

The Beast stepped out of the shadows by the door, and the light of all the lamps in the room fell on his face. Belle's hands flew to cover her eyes, to shield them from the hideous sight, and it was with great difficulty that at last she peeped between her fingers at the Beast.

'Now,' he said, 'are you as ready as you were a moment ago to spend your days with me?'

Belle was quiet for a full minute, then she said, 'I will become used to looking at you, sir, and then I will not flinch as I did just now. You must forgive me for my cruelty. It was the unexpectedness of seeing you for the first time. I shall not hide my eyes again.'

The Beast bowed. 'You are as kind as you are beautiful. Everything I own, everything in this place is yours to do with as you will. I shall keep out of your sight, except for one hour in the evening, when I will come into the drawing-room for some conversation. For the present, I beg the two of you to enjoy this last night together, for tomorrow your father must leave and return home. I bid you both goodnight.'

The next morning, after her father had gone, Belle wept for a long time. Then she dried her eyes and said to herself, 'Crying will not help me, nor despair. I must strive to enjoy everything there is to enjoy, and find the courage to endure whatever I have to endure.'

She decided to explore the mansion, and found that everything she looked at had been designed to please her. There were books in the library, a piano in the music room, paints and pencils for her amusement, a wardrobe full of the most beautiful clothes that anyone could wish for, and everywhere invisible hands that made all ready for her and smoothed her way.

Beside her bed, on a small table, there lay a looking-glass and a note which read:

'Whatever you may wish to see
will in this glass reflected be.'

Belle picked up the little mirror and wished that she might see her family and know how they fared, but the images that appeared made her so homesick, that at once she put the glass away in a drawer and tried to forget all about it.

And so Belle passed her days pleasantly enough, and every evening as the clock struck nine, the Beast came and sat beside her in the drawing-room.

At first, Belle dreaded this time, and the sound of the Beast's footsteps on the marble floors made her tremble with fear. But when he sat down, his face was in shadow, and as they talked, Belle's fears melted away, and the hour passed too quickly. Soon, she began to long for the evening, and to wish that she might spend time with the Beast during the day.

One night, as the candles guttered and flickered, the Beast stood up to take his leave of her.

Belle whispered, 'Stay a little longer, sir. It is very lonely and quiet without you, and this hour is so short.'

The Beast sat down again, and said, 'I will gladly stay for as long as you wish, but there is a question I must ask you and I shall ask this question every night and you must answer me honestly.'

'I would never lie to you, sir,' said Belle, 'for you are the best and most generous of creatures.'

'Then tell me, Belle, would you consent to marry me?'

'Oh, no, sir!' cried Belle, and her hands flew to her mouth and she shuddered in disgust. 'No, I could never marry you. I am sorry to say this after all your kindness to me, but oh, no, do not ask such a thing of me, I implore you!'

The Beast turned away from the light.

'I apologize for causing you distress,' he said, 'but I must ask this question every night.'

Time went by. Belle and the Beast spoke of everything: of dreams and songs and poems and flowers and wars and noble deeds and merriment. They spoke of wizards and dragons and magic and marvels, of clouds and mountains and distant empires. They discussed kings and emperors, architecture and farming, families and animals. The only subject they never mentioned was love.

And still, as he left her side, the Beast asked every night, 'Will you marry me, Belle?' and Belle would say that she could not.

At first she said it in words, but gradually, uttering the syllables that hurt the Beast so much began to hurt her too, and she found herself unable to speak. After that, she simply shook her head and her heart grew heavier and heavier.

One night, after Belle had spent nearly a year and a half in the Beast's house, she took the enchanted mirror out of the drawer, and asked to be shown her family at home. What she saw was an old man lying sick and feverish in his bed. She could scarcely recognize her dear father, who had been so tall and strong and who had seemed to her so young. She wept bitterly at the sight.

'I shall ask the Master to let me visit him,' she decided. 'He would not refuse me such a favour.'

That evening, Belle wept again as she told the Beast of her father's illness.

'If you let me go to him, I promise to come back within the week, only I cannot bear to see him suffering.'

'And I cannot bear to see *you* suffering, my dear one. Take this magic ring with you, and place it on your finger when you wish to return to this place. All you have to do to be in your father's house is look into the mirror and wish yourself transported.'

'Thank you, thank you, dear sir,' said Belle. 'I shall be back with you before you can miss me.'

'And will you marry me, dearest Belle?'

'No, sir,' said Belle. 'You know I could never do that.'

'Then goodnight,' said the Beast, 'and may you find whatever it is you seek.'

The next morning, Belle woke up in her father's house. His happiness at her return was so great that his health immediately improved, and even Belle's sisters were glad to see her. But every night at nine o'clock, Belle found her thoughts turning to the Beast, and she missed their conversations together and their shared laughter.

When the week was over, she was quite ready to leave, but her father's piteous tears persuaded her and she agreed to stay with her family for a few more days. 'The Master will not mind,' she said to herself, 'for he is so kind and gentle.'

On the third night of the second week, Belle dreamed of the rose garden. She saw in her dream the very bush from which her father had taken the red rose she had asked for, and under the bush lay the Master. His voice came to her from far away.

'I am dying, Belle,' she heard. 'Dying for love of you. I cannot live even one more day if you do not come back. You have broken your promise to me, and thus broken my heart . . .'

Belle awoke from the dream at once, cold and terrified.

Quickly, she put on the magic ring and lay back against the pillows.

'Take me back to him,' she told the ring, and tears poured from her eyes. 'What if I am too late and my Master is dead? Oh, let me be in time. Please let me be in time!'

Belle opened her eyes and she was once more in her bedroom in the mansion. Without even pausing to put slippers on her feet, she ran through the corridors and down the stairs and out of the front door. Breathless, she came to the rose garden, and there on the ground lay the Beast, silent and unmoving. Belle flung herself upon him and took him in her arms.

'Oh, Master, please, please do not die. I cannot, I cannot be too late. How will I ever bear it if you die? Oh, can you not feel my love for you? Come back to life and I will do anything . . . I will marry you gladly, joyously – only speak to me, I beseech you.'

Belle's tears fell on the Beast's hair as she kissed his eyes and clasped him to her heart. At last he stirred and Belle looked down at him for the first time. She found she was embracing a handsome young man, and recoiled at once.

'You are not my beloved Master,' she cried. 'Where is he? I love him. I want to marry him.'

'Don't you recognize me?' asked the young man, who indeed did speak with the Beast's own voice. 'Don't you know me without the mask of my ugliness? It is I, and you will never call me Master again, but Husband and Friend. I am the same as I ever was, and love you as much as I ever did. You have released me from a dreadful spell laid upon me in childhood by a wicked fairy who was envious of my wealth. She turned me into a monster until the day a woman would agree to marry me. Can you love me, Belle, as I really am?'

'I will love you,' said Belle. 'I *do* love you. I have loved you for a long time, though I did not realize it until last night. I love your face, whether it be beautiful or hideous, for it is your face and only an outer shell for your honourable soul.'

'Then we shall be happy for ever,' said the young man. 'And the whole world will dance at our wedding.'

Belle smiled and took his hand, and they entered their home together.

Brian and the Brain

SARA VOGLER AND JANET BURCHETT

Brian had homework. It was writing, and writing was a bit of a problem for Brian. Whatever he produced, it would look as if a drunken spider had staggered across the page. Whatever he produced, he knew what Miss Spenshaw would say.

'It may be the best work in the history of the school, Brian, but as I can't read it we shall never know, shall we? Perhaps we could fax it off to Beijing for a translation.'

There's nothing like a good joke, thought Brian, and that's nothing like a good joke.

Of course, there would be no problem if he could do it on the computer. But last week, while he'd been trying to install *Attack of the Killer Klingfilms*, Mum's story *Ellie and the Elves Go Skipping* had somehow got deleted. She'd been about to send it off to her publisher. Brian felt it was unfair. Mum had claimed that it was his fault. But the whole family knew what the computer was like. An eccentric, cranky old thing. Second-hand from the eccentric cranky old woman down the road, 'The Brain' had come into the family like an intelligent but unreliable dog. You never knew if it was going to lick, bite or wee on the carpet. You touched it at your peril. Dad wouldn't go near it. Not since the mouse had given him an electric shock.

The Brain had no sense of humour. In the face of the most ridiculous spelling mistake it would merely add a solemn red line underneath. It ignored Brian's expertise at space games – even when he got top of the top ten. And sometimes it would announce unexpectedly that you had performed an illegal operation and the program would now be closed down or else. Brian often wondered what it would do – send the computer police round? He thought about what they would look like. Would they knock politely or beat your door down?

But when The Brain swallowed Ellie, along with

twenty-four of her elfin friends, Brian's mother had gently discouraged him from using it for a while.

'If you ever touch that machine again, I will personally come into your assembly and read *Ellie and the Elves Go to the Farm* – with sound effects.'

So Brian thought he would give technology a miss for a few days.

But this was serious. The homework had to be in tomorrow. Otherwise, Miss Spenshaw had said, he could do it during football practice. Luckily, Mum was out in the garden having a fight with the ivy. She'd be ages. The ivy always won in the end. There was plenty of time to finish a game of *Space Bowls* and thrash out the homework too.

But first he had to put the wet sponges in Grace's bed and stick the plastic spider on her mirror. It was nearly a week since he'd glued her shoes to the bedroom floor. He mustn't let standards slip. When he got back to the computer he felt that a quick game of *Space Bowls* would loosen up his fingers nicely. He made level thirty-seven before being blown to pieces. Not bad. Now for the essay. Or should he have a quick game of *Giant Aphids of Andromeda?* No, he must be strong. He resigned himself to the unpleasant task ahead.

'All About Me'. How stupid. It was like being five again. Why couldn't Miss Spenshaw let him write about 'How to be world champion at *Marauding Martians*'? Or, 'My Hundred Best Practical Jokes'? He sighed, slumped down in his seat and typed:

<u>all abot me bye Brain Bossley</u>

PlEase see work done 6 weeks ago when yoooooooou were off with the chicken pox and WE HaD thAt naFF SUPPLy teacher who kept falling aSleep. zzzzzzzzzzzzzz. i haven't cHanGEd snincE then. i thank you.

He looked up and read what he'd written. Keyboard skills were not his strong point but at least she'd be able to read it. The Brain had put red lines under nearly every word. Brian ignored them. He didn't need keyboard skills, not when he was so ace with the mouse and the joystick. Then he remembered. He had to finish with 'My Greatest Wish'. He'd make them all laugh. He thought he might wish to be Mike Megabyte, hero of *Alien Bashers Anon*. He stared at the screen. He noticed he'd spelt his name wrong – Brain. That was it! Never mind Mike Megabyte, he'd have the lot. He'd have the entire brain of the computer. He'd reach level 1027 of *Thundering Terrapins* before they knew what had hit them. He wouldn't have to struggle with his handwriting. He might even find maths easier if he could understand it. And he'd probably make even quicker quips. Yes, he'd have them rolling in the aisles. He'd probably get into *The Guinness Book of Records* – the Boy with a Brain the Size of Jupiter. But that sort of thing only happened in *Nova-nerds from Neptune* where you picked up extra brain-power as you went along. Slipping further down in his seat, he carried on typing.

`i wish to swOp brains with my cOmpouter.`

He grabbed the mouse to click on 'print'. But the moment he did so he felt a weird sensation in his head. It was as if someone had flushed his brain. He could feel it emptying like a toilet cistern. Then, an army of electronic ants seemed to march from the mouse, into his fingers, up his arm and finally into his skull.

The back door banged.

'What are you up to, Brian?' shouted Mum. 'I hope you're not on that computer.'

Brian mechanically tidied up the computer table, tucked in the chair and marched up to bed without a word.

Next morning, Mum came in to give Brian the first of his time checks and increasingly unpleasant threats. She pulled back the curtains.

'Welcome to Windows,' said a loud voice behind

her. She swung round. Brian was standing, fully dressed, beside an immaculately made bed. Mum couldn't believe it. She staggered out. Brian, feeling rather odd, marched down to breakfast behind her.

He stared at his cereal.

'There are two hundred and fifty-six Corn Crunchies in my bowl. The square root of two hundred and fifty-six is sixteen. Therefore it will only take me sixteen spoonfuls of sixteen Corn Crunchies to finish my cereal – with no remainder.'

'That was impressive, Brian,' said Dad when he'd checked the arithmetic on the back of an envelope. He looked at his son. 'Are you OK, Brian? You're looking a bit pale.'

Brian considered this. He certainly did feel different this morning. And more surprisingly still, he found he wasn't interested in retrieving the spider and sponges before Grace threw them away. That all seemed rather childish and totally irrelevant now. But then, of course, when you had 1.6 gigabytes and 100 megahertz who needed jokes and space games? Maths, data, memory – that was the real world.

'Brian can't even add up,' said his sister grumpily. She'd had a bad night. 'He's got a brain the size of a Ricicle. He must've got it off the back of the cereal packet. I'm fed up with Corn Crunchies, Mum. Haven't we got anything else?'

'Did you know,' Brian piped up to his own surprise, 'just one click brings down a menu?'

His family ignored him. They were used to his jokes.

'One of these days,' Mum was saying to anyone who would listen, 'I'm going wallpaper shopping. I'm fed up with these spots. If I don't watch out, I'm going to find myself counting them . . .'

'There are two million, one hundred and sixty thousand, three hundred and thirty-seven spots on the kitchen walls,' announced Brian. Mum put her hand on his forehead.

'Are you feeling all right, Brian?' she asked.

'Everything is in normal view, thank you,' said Brian. 'And please call me Brain.'

He marched off to school.

Brian sat at his table. He laid out his pens, rulers and rubbers in neat rows. He finally managed to find his books in the clutter of his drawer, and arranged them symmetrically in front of him. Now he had customized his desktop he looked up – ready and waiting to impress.

'Brian Bossley,' said Miss Spenshaw sternly, 'if it's not too much to ask, could I have your homework please?'

'The file cannot be found,' said Brian, staring

squarely at her. 'Please check that the correct file name has been entered.'

The class began to titter. Brian, the school clown, never failed. And more impressive, Brian was keeping a straight face.

'That's enough, Brian,' said Miss Spenshaw. 'I want to see "All About Me" – NOW!'

'Correct file name has been entered,' replied Brian. 'Ready to print. And please call me Brain.'

The class giggled. But for some reason Brian didn't look round with his usual merry grin. Miss Spenshaw stared. She hadn't expected him to do as he was told. Brian hadn't expected to do as he was told either. But he had to – she had issued a command.

He took a clean sheet of paper and carefully sharpened a pencil. He did a mental spell check, sorted out the capital letters and completed a word count. He wondered why he had written this rubbish. It was pathetic for a boy with a brain the size of Jupiter.

'File name "All About Me" . . . font – extremely untidy . . . double space . . . font size – overlarge, twenty-six.'

With the speed of a printer, his work appeared on the paper. Only the ending had changed:

'Computers have no need for wishes, only commands. Tip of the day - did you know

you can speed up your working efficiency with extra megabytes?'

With that, Brian suddenly got up and walkcd round the classroom collecting all the books. He put them into brown folders.

'What are you doing?' asked Miss Spenshaw.

'All work has now been saved in files,' announced Brian. The class started laughing.

'Good old Brian,' said Luke. 'He never fails.'

Brian felt a surge of irritation.

'Please call me Brain,' he snapped.

Meanwhile at home, Mum switched on the computer to do some work. The machine made a dreadful grinding noise.

'Wotcha!' read the screen.

Mum was surprised. Brian must have learnt how to customize the screen saver at last.

'Beep!'

The whole class jumped. Brian didn't usually go in for beeping.

'To gracebossley from williamwigeon@stevenage birdsanctuary.co.uk. Spoonbills safely hatched. Mother and chicks doing well,' Brian announced.

Everyone fell about. Gradually the laughter died

down as the kids realized that Brian wasn't joking. Brian ignored them and carried on with his maths.

'Brian . . . Brian!'

'Ready, Miss Spenshaw.'

'Thank you for sharing that with us, Brian. Perhaps you will kindly explain yourself.'

'Just delivering an e-mail message. And please call me Brain.'

Miss Spenshaw walked over and peered at Brian's work. Her jaw dropped down to her knees. Although it was as untidy as ever, it was all correct and he was on page twenty-two already.

Mum wasn't getting much work done. Ellie and the Elves hadn't finished packing their picnic basket yet. She had hoped to get them to the woods before lunch. She kept being interrupted by prompt boxes:

? What's for tea?

and

! This story is soooooo bor-ing!

and

? Have you heard the one about the rabbit and the spirit level?

The computer had even called her 'mum' twice and claimed it was too tired to do any work. Mum wished she had gone wallpaper shopping instead.

At breaktime, Luke skidded up to Brian, hands out ready for the usual joystick wrist-actions and synchronized air-mousing. But Brian ignored him. He'd only been out there for three minutes and forty-eight point nine seconds and he'd already been pestered six times by children asking him to tell them jokes. No one wanted Encarta. No one needed a bar chart. No one even asked after his database. He wanted to fulfil commands, save, edit, insert and take messages. He wanted to show them what he could do.

'Beep! To mrjohnbossley from robbie.reliant @dodgymotors.co.uk. Ford Capri E reg. Excellent condition. Egg yellow with green doors . . .'

'You're no fun any more, Brian Bossley,' said Luke. 'Your jokes are awful – and you've turned into a boffin.'

Brian considered the matter.

'Boffin. Not found in thesaurus. Suggest change to bodkin or bog.'

'You swot!' shouted Luke.

'Swot,' said Brian. 'No synonyms found. And please call me Brain.'

Luke stormed off. Brian stood there, blinking.

Then, from somewhere deep down came an illogical thought. Brian ignored it at first. He thought it was the screen saver scrolling across his vision.

Call Luke back and tell him it's all a joke. Call Luke back and tell him . . .

Brian tried to delete it but it wouldn't go. It kept on scrolling. It bothered him. It rattled his RAM.

Mum had gone past the point of calling the computer words you wouldn't find in any spell check. Now she sat there in silence. She was even thinking about writing her story by hand. The computer had given up its irritating messages, but now her entire story had gone missing. She searched frantically and finally found it. She opened the file. Up came the title – *Ellie and the Elves Get Beaten Up*. There followed grisly descriptions of packs of avenging pixies and disembowelled elves hanging from trees. Then a prompt box appeared.

! Well that's disposed of Ellie and the Elves. Let's play *Vlad the Inhaler*. It's a bit of a wheeze. You'll like it if you try it, Mum !

'Just wait till I get my hands on that boy,' muttered Brian's mother.

By quarter past eleven, Brian had finished his year's work.

'Beep!'

'Brian, stop that!'

'To mrsevangelinebossley from r.t.choke@veg-u-like.recipes.co.uk. Spinach and Aubergine Burger. First chop the spinach. Then soak the aubergines in orange juice . . .'

'I suppose he thinks that's funny,' Luke called out. 'But it's not. He's lost his sense of humour.'

Brian tried to access C:\Sense.of.humour. No file found. It bothered him. He kept searching. Another message unexpectedly scrolled across.

`Why aren't they laughing any more? Why aren't they laughing . . .`

Brian, the boy with a brain the size of Jupiter, couldn't understand why this was so important to him. But somehow it was. If he couldn't sort it out he might have to shut down – and then what?

'Beep!'

He didn't want to give the next message but he couldn't stop himself.

'To miss.cuddlekins.spenshaw from your tiger.-cyril.blake@county.high.school.uk . . .'

'Brian! I'm warning you!'

'Looking forward to our date tonight and lots of snoodling . . .'

'Brian. Go to the office at once and tell them to take your temperature.'

Brian marched to the office. When he got there, Mrs Thompson, the school secretary, was updating the database. He stepped purposefully forward to assist. Instead a thermometer was inserted in his mouth.

'Keep still and don't bite it,' said Mrs Thompson.

Brian sat on the sick chair. He wanted to sort out this strange feeling. It did not compute properly. He didn't like his megabytes being muddled. Having the brain of a computer wasn't half as good as he'd thought. There was something seriously wrong. A brain the size of Jupiter was all very well but there was something missing.

I feel lonely. Where are my friends? I feel lonely. Where are my friends?

came the message from somewhere. Brian checked his hard drive for an error. The message changed.

I can't stand this any more. I can't stand this any more. I can't stand this . . .

Now he knew what the problem was. Brian was rejecting The Brain. He needed to be Brian, King Joker and Champion Space Bowler. He tried to make contact with the home terminal. He announced the message.

'Beep! Brianswop/genius.2.idiot. Urgent. Find conversion files. Matter of life and shutdown.'

'Burp! Brianswop\idiot.2.genius,' came the reply. 'Who are you calling an idiot? Who wasted his time going to school? And who gave Ellie a thrashing and played games all day? Convert? Get lost!'

Mrs Thompson watched Brian open-mouthed. She reached for the telephone.

'Mrs Bossley? It's Susan Thompson at Rembrandt School.'

Hysterical cackles could be heard at the other end of the line. 'Can you come and fetch Brian? I think he has a virus . . . What do you mean, he'd be safer at school? No, I haven't got a sledge-hammer handy.' She put the phone down rather quickly.

'Mummy won't be long, dear . . . Or perhaps I should phone Daddy?'

When he got home, Brian tottered weakly towards the computer.

'System failure imminent,' he muttered. 'System failure imminent.'

But Mum got there first. She barred his way.

'Get away from it,' she shrieked. 'I've had enough of your jokes.'

She shoved a couple of paracetamol into his hand.

'Go and lie down. I'm phoning the help line . . .'

Brian sank down in the corner as she dialled.

'. . . Hello? Hello! Yes it's me again . . . I can't access any files, and when I do, they've been changed. My deadline is Friday and my elves have been brutally murdered . . . Yes, I have got the right number . . . Wait, I haven't finished yet! The computer thinks I'm its mother and it wants me to play games . . . What? No, I am not on any medication.' She slammed the phone down. 'Where's the manual? I'm going to complain.'

She stormed out.

Brian dragged himself to his feet and sank down at the computer. He had to do it before she got back. He opened 'all abot me'. He could hear Mum throwing books about in the lounge. He scrolled down quickly to the end of the text. Then he heard Mum's footsteps. She was coming back. He deleted the last two lines and typed

I want to be Brian again.

Mum opened the door. Brian grabbed the mouse. He felt the bytes emptying down his arm and rushing back to the computer.

A prompt box suddenly came up on the screen.

`On your bike. I'm staying put . . .`

For a moment Brian thought he was going to pass out. But then the message slowly faded and a sloppy, bubbly feeling sloshed up into his brain as if he was being filled with lemonade.

He smiled.

'BRIAN!'

Mum leaped at him and tried to grab the mouse. An army of electronic ants seemed to march from the mouse, into her fingers, up her arm and finally into her skull.

Mum began skipping round the room. Brian watched her in amazement. She danced out into the kitchen. She picked up a tea-towel and tied it around her head like a scarf. Then she took a basket. She filled it with sandwiches, cake and a bottle of pop.

'What a lovely day for a picnic!' she chirped as she opened the back door. Then she seemed to change her mind. She laid down the basket and went over to the kitchen cupboard. She brought out a large wooden rolling-pin.

'Mum!' said Brian, 'What are you doing?'

'I'm going to sort out those pixies once and for all,' she muttered. 'And please call me Ellie.'

A Matter of Time

Sue Welford

Amita lay motionless, the faraway thunder of the explosion still echoing in her ears. She coughed, choking on the dry, biting dust. Her eyes stung. Something warm and sticky ran down her forehead and over her closed, terrified eyelids.

When at last she opened her eyes, Amita could see nothing. Clouds of pink dust swirled around her like a sandstorm. Tentatively, she raised her head. She moved her arm to wipe away the stickiness from her face. Looking down, she saw it was blood. She lay still, still as death, hardly even daring to breathe.

A few metres away, Jonathan Holroyd struggled to

sit up. Dull light from the below-pavement-level window made routes through the swirling dust. Jonathan could just make out a metal girder resting against a pile of shattered bricks. The end of the girder was across his leg. His fingers reached out and clasped something. When he brought his hand into view, he saw it was a Barbie doll. Her silver cocktail dress was torn and tattered. Half her face was gone. Somewhere in the distance Jonathan thought he heard a scream.

Carefully, Jonathan tried to withdraw his foot. Immediately, an agonizing, searing pain shot up his leg. He yelled. The air seemed to spin and hover in front of him. Dizzy with pain, he lay back on the hard, rubble-strewn floor and began to cry. Hot tears made rivers in the dry dust on his face. He could hear the insistent drip, drip of water from a fractured pipe.

'Who is it . . . who's there?'

It sounded like a girl. Jonathan wiped the moisture from his cheeks, feeling the scratchy plaster score his skin. He sniffed. There was a smell. Something nasty – a metallic kind of smell. Jonathan sneezed. The dust was beginning to clear now, settling on the ruined basement floor of the department store. He sat up again. Slowly this time. He took a deep breath and the world stopped spinning.

Across the fallen beam he could just make out a figure. It was lying on the ground, covered with large fragments of plaster.

'It's me!' Jonathan cried. He tried to move but fell back, pain shrieking up his leg.

The voice came again. Weak but perfectly clear.

'Who's me?'

'Jonathan . . .'

'Where are you, Jonathan? I can't see you.'

'I'm here.'

Jonathan saw the figure move, begin to turn over. As it did so, there was a deep rumble and not far away another beam fell with a crash. Clouds of dust and debris rose like an eruption. A tangle of twisted metal fell from above, bouncing like a crazy, agonized spider.

Jonathan froze. Then he whispered hoarsely, 'I think you'd better stay still.'

The voice came back to him. 'Yes.'

There was silence for a little while. Miles away, Jonathan could hear the scream of sirens and deep rumbles that seemed to come from the bowels of the earth.

A bit later, the girl's voice came again.

'Are you OK, Jonathan?'

'I . . . I think so. My leg's stuck under this beam thing. It . . . it really hurts.' Jonathan felt the tears come again. He brushed them away. If only he hadn't insisted on being 'grown up' and gone down to the basement to get his dad's Christmas present by himself, everything would have been all right. He patted his coat pocket. The present for his dad was still there, safe, not at all squashed. The feel of the small box gave him a sense of reassurance.

He heard the girl again. 'Best not to try to move, Jonathan. I'm sure someone will come to rescue us soon.'

'They won't know we're here.'

'Yes they will. Someone will . . .'

'Where are your mum and dad?' Jonathan asked.

'At home. Mum told me not to come shopping. She said they'd threatened a bombing campaign . . .'

'Do you think that's what it was then . . .?'

'I don't know . . . Where are your parents, Jonathan?'

Jonathan sniffed. His leg was going numb now, right up to the top. 'They've gone next door to the Pizza Hut to wait for me. I was just getting my dad's present, then we were going to have dinner.'

'I expect they'll be all right then.'

'Yes . . .'

Jonathan saw the figure shift again, awkwardly, like a puppet that had lost its strings. 'They'll know where you are. They'll tell the rescuers.'

'I hope the rescuers come soon.' Jonathan sniffed again. There was still that funny smell. He'd smelt it before somewhere but couldn't think where.

'They will, Jonathan. They'll be looking already. I know they will.'

'What's your name?' Jonathan called.

'Amita.'

'What do you think has happened to the others, Amita?'

'What others?'

'The other people who were looking at the toys and the sports stuff next door. There was a lady with a baby in a pram . . .' Jonathan didn't want to think about it.

There was another small silence. 'I don't know.' Then Amita called, 'Is anyone else there . . .? Anyone else . . . alive?'

Only silence answered. Jonathan couldn't even hear the sirens any more.

'Jonathan?'

'Yes . . .' Jonathan sniffed, crying silently with fear and pain.

'I'm going to try to get over to you.'

'OK . . . No . . . you'd better not.' Jonathan looked up fearfully. Above his head, cables and wires swung precariously. There was a great, jagged hole in the ceiling. Brightly coloured ladies' clothes hung through like ragged washing. It looked as if the whole lot might come down at any minute.

Jonathan heard a kind of scraping sound. He turned his head sideways. Someone who looked like a scarecrow was crawling towards him. The figure pushed away a pile of boxes with spaceships inside, moved gingerly beneath a fallen beam. At last it reached him.

It was the girl, although you'd never have known it. She had pink, dusty hair. It looked as if it had once been woven into a single, thick plait down the back. Blood was running down her face. It made roadways down her cheek and you could see the dark skin beneath the pale dust. One earlobe was torn and bloody, the other held a gold ring. There was a long rent in her tracksuit trousers. Jonathan could see blood there too.

As she reached him, the girl put out her hand and clutched his. Then she managed a kind of wobbly smile. There was so little room she could hardly even sit up properly. She just lay beside him, clutching on to his hand as if it was a life-line.

After a few minutes, the girl pushed back a lock of hair that had escaped from its plait. She gazed down, with a shocked expression on her face. A handful had come out in her fingers. The blood began to ooze again. Her dark eyes were wide in her dusty face.

'Your head's smashed up,' Jonathan said, feeling sick.

She managed another smile; her teeth and gums looked yellow against her grimy skin.

'It's OK. Scalp wounds always bleed a lot. I learned that at Red Cross.'

'What are we going to do?' Jonathan asked, tears welling again in his eyes.

'We'll just have to wait until they come.' The girl squeezed his hand tightly. 'It'll be all right, Jonathan. People always get rescued.'

Jonathan rubbed his nose with the back of his hand. 'No they don't.'

'Well . . . we're going to be, so don't worry. We'll just wait here and when we hear them coming, we'll shout. OK?'

'OK,' Jonathan sniffed.

'Does your leg hurt?' Amita asked.

'Only when I try to move. It feels numb . . . up here.' Jonathan rubbed his groin.

'Do you think it's broken?'

'I don't know.'

'If it wasn't trapped under that beam I could probably tell if it was. We did it at Red Cross. I could make a splint . . .'

Jonathan didn't answer. There didn't seem to be any point in talking about it. His leg was stuck and that was that.

'Were you doing your Christmas shopping?'

'We don't really have a proper Christmas,' Amita said. 'I was watching a lady do a cookery demonstration upstairs and I'd just come down to look at the toys . . . it's my sister's birthday soon.'

'Oh . . .' Jonathan couldn't really think what it would be like, not having a proper Christmas.

They lay in silence. Jonathan began to shiver. He felt sick again. It was that horrible smell . . .

'What's that smell, Amita?'

'I don't know.'

'It's horrible.'

'Yes.'

Jonathan's teeth were chattering. He felt a movement beside him. He opened his eyes to see Amita struggling to take off her tracksuit top. She put it over him, tucking it round his chin as if he was a baby. Then she lay close to him again. She put her arm across his chest. He could smell the faint aroma of perspiration. Of fear.

Warmer, he felt better.

The light from the window gradually faded. Soon it was pitch dark. Silent. Even the steady drip of the fractured water pipe had ceased. Jonathan thought about his mum, his dad. They'd come up to London for the day, Christmas shopping. Mum said she was glad to get away for a bit. Some men had been digging the road up outside their house for weeks and she was fed up with the mess.

'They've all gone home,' Jonathan whispered. 'They've given up looking.'

Amita shook her head. 'No, they won't do that. I've seen it on television – when bombs go off and earthquakes and things. They always look for ages and ages.'

Jonathan didn't know how, but he must have fallen asleep. Wild nightmares haunted his brain. Once, he awoke, hearing a cry. Then he realized it was coming from him. Beside him, Amita hugged him close.

'It's OK, Jonathan,' she murmured. 'They'll be here soon.'

He began to cry again. His throat was so dry he thought he was going to choke. A vision of a cool McDonald's vanilla milkshake floated before his eyes – a vision so clear he could almost feel the thick, creamy taste on his tongue. He felt ashamed. A big boy of eight – crying. His mum had always told him it was all right for boys to cry too – it wasn't only girls who were allowed. He felt ashamed all the same. Crying wouldn't do any good at all.

Jonathan awoke finally to a new orchestra of sound. Light was streaming through the shattered, jagged panes in the basement window. He could hear a faint, insistent tap-tapping above his head. There was a sharp ring of a hammer hitting metal and the deep, rhythmic hum of a compressor somewhere in the road.

He nudged Amita.

'Amita, wake up.'

The girl turned stiffly. She sat up, then groaned, putting her hand to her head.

Turning, she smiled. 'What . . .?'

'That noise . . .'

Amita cocked her head to one side. 'It's them,' she said. 'I knew they'd come.' She coughed, trying to clear her throat. Then she shouted, 'We're here! Help! We're here!'

But her shouting dislodged some of the plaster from the ceiling. It fell down like pink, choking snow. Then a big lump fell, striking her on the shoulder. Jonathan clutched her arm.

'Don't,' he hissed. 'Don't.' Jonathan could hardly bear to look. Supposing that other beam fell down on top of them; supposing that cracked wall caved in . . .

They waited . . . And waited . . . After a while, the tapping stopped.

'They've gone,' Jonathan whispered, his voice trembling. 'They've gone.'

Amita took hold of his arms. 'Jonathan, you've got to be brave!'

'I'm trying,' he sobbed.

'And you're doing very well. I've got a little brother about your age. He wouldn't be nearly as brave as you're being . . . but you mustn't give up. OK?'

Jonathan wiped his nose with the back of his hand. 'OK.'

Amita began to talk to him then. She told him about her house and her brothers and sisters. About her father who owned a shop and her mother who helped out, serving people from behind the counter. She told him about her grandmother and grandfather who had come from a place called Uganda when there was a war. They'd had to hide from a cruel dictator who was killing everyone. They had come to live in England so their children could grow up safely. They had been *really* brave, she told him. They'd arrived with nothing but the clothes they stood up in.

'Tell me about your family, Jonathan.'

'There's me and my mum and dad,' Jonathan told her.

'What do they do?'

'My mum works at home. She sews curtains and things.'

'What about your dad?'

'He works in an office and . . .' Jonathan brightened up a bit. 'He's a football referee too . . . do you like football?'

Amita grinned. 'Yes, it's great.'

Jonathan was beginning to feel tired again. All he wanted to do was go to sleep. His leg was beginning to hurt again, too. He must have moved in the night and twisted it. He closed his eyes.

Amita nudged him. 'Hey, Jonathan, you'd better not go to sleep.'

'Why not,' he mumbled.

'In case the rescuers come back.'

'I don't care.'

'Jonathan . . . Jonathan . . .'

From way above there came a rumble, then the sound of falling masonry. There was the noise of a hammer again and a machine of some kind. It sounded like one of those big diggers used on building sites.

'Jonny, Jonny, they've come back. They've got a machine. Listen . . .'

As Amita spoke, a large beam above their heads moved to one side. Electricity cables snapped, sparking like fireworks.

Jonathan struggled to sit up. 'No . . . no, they mustn't move anything else, they mustn't!'

Amita looked up fearfully. 'It's all right, it's stuck against that pillar. I don't think it's going to fall . . .'

'No,' Jonathan cried. 'It's the sparks.'

'It's OK, they're not near enough to hurt us.'

'Amita, don't you see . . .' Jonathan said urgently.

'It's that smell. I've remembered what it is. It's gas.'

'Gas!'

'Yes, they've been digging up the road outside our house to lay pipes. There was a leak or something. It smelt just like that!'

'Oh, no!' Amita looked up at the naked, dangling wire, still sparking. She wiped the back of her hand across her brow. Jonathan could see she was sweating – fear like crystals in the palm of her hand.

A lump of masonry fell with a crash. Rubble scattered. The girder imprisoning Jonathan's leg moved slightly. He screamed and covered his head with his arms.

'No! Stop!' Amita shouted, looking up again, panic-stricken. 'Stop . . . you'll kill us. Please!'

Somewhere above, the machine rumbled on . . . and on . . .

After a minute, Amita spoke again.

'Jon! Jon!'

Jonathan looked at her.

'Jon, we've got to let them know we're here. Make them stop digging.'

Jonathan shook his head. 'How? They haven't heard us shouting, they're making too much noise.'

The smell was getting stronger now. As if the shifting beam had opened up the broken pipe more than ever.

Jonathan could see Amita sitting with her head in her hands. She fumbled in the pocket of her tracksuit trousers and gave him a hanky. 'Here,' she said, 'hold this over your nose.'

'No.' Jonathan put his hand into his own pocket. 'I've got one, you use yours.'

Out with his hanky tumbled the present he'd bought for his dad.

'Jonny . . .' Amita had tied a scarf round her face like cowboys did in those old Western movies Jonathan's dad liked.

He tried to do the same. As Amita helped him, she said, 'Jonny, see that gap over there?'

Jonathan turned his head. Across, by the exit, a gap had opened up in the ruined wall. 'Yes,' he said, his voice muffled by the handkerchief. He could still smell the gas, even through the material.

'I'm going to try to get over there.'

'I don't think you should. You'll knock something . . . or that cable might fall on top of you.'

'I've got to, Jonathan . . . before it's too late.'

'All right.' Jonathan lay back with a sigh. He didn't really care what Amita did. They were going to die in here and that was that. If they didn't get blown up or electrocuted, they'd be squashed to death by bricks and stuff. It was only a matter of time.

The girl shook him. 'Jonathan, wake up. I need you.'

'What for?'

'To warn me if anything starts moving again.'

'I can't.'

'Yes you can . . . Sit up. Now!'

Jonathan sat up. Amita gave him a hug. He could smell the dry, plaster-filled dust on her face and hair. She left him and began to crawl across the floor. Her body left a trail in the dirt and rubble. Jonathan saw her move a great piece of cracked concrete to one side. A pile of boxes trembled, then fell on top of her. She brushed them aside impatiently. In front of the newly opened gap, a doll's pram rested on its side, twisted and smashed almost beyond recognition. Jonathan thought again of the lady with the pram who had been standing beside him looking at the racing-car models. He'd seen her before, asking the assistant about the golf clubs. He remembered she had smiled at him and the baby had chuckled . . .

The severed head of a rocking horse lay near the broken pram.

When Amita reached the gap, she turned. She lifted her arm and waved.

'I made it, Jonny.'

'Yes,' he called.

'You OK?'

'Yes.' He didn't know if she heard him. His voice sounded so weak and peculiar it was as if it belonged to someone else. He wished like anything that he could have a drink of water.

'Help!' Amita put her head between two criss-cross fallen girders. She shouted through the gap. 'Help us! Please!'

She turned. Even through the gloom, Jonathan could see desperation on her grimy face.

'It's no good,' she called. 'It's hopeless. We could be down here for days and they wouldn't ever know.'

Jonathan suddenly remembered something he'd seen on television. Pictures of people being found in the wreckage of buildings, not only days after they'd been buried, but weeks sometimes. The rescuers had got dogs, trained especially to sniff people out. Jonathan liked dogs. His dad had a dog when he was a boy, but Jonathan's mum said they made too much mess. 'He was great . . . Rusty, he was called,' Jonathan's dad had said. 'Ever so good. I trained him with a special . . .'

Jonathan's hand closed over the little box by his side.

'Amita,' he called urgently. 'Amita, come here!'

Amita crawled slowly back to him. She put her arm across his shoulders. She took the hanky from her face. The ruined basement seemed to echo with the thunder of the overhead machine. All around them dust and debris began falling. Then, suddenly, the machine stopped.

Jonathan saw tears in Amita's dark eyes. 'I'm sorry, Jonathan.'

Jonathan thrust the box into her hand. 'Look!' he said. 'Take this . . . my dad won't mind if it's been used. Quick, before they start that thing up again.'

Amita brushed her tears away impatiently. Then a slow grin spread across her face when she saw what Jonathan had given her.

Carefully, slowly, Amita crawled back to the gap. She tore open the box and lifted something to her lips. She took a deep breath. A shrill whistle rang out. The sound seemed to bounce round the basement, out through the gap and up towards the rescuers above.

Jonathan wrenched off the handkerchief. If Amita could be brave, then so could he. Eyeing the sparking cable warily, he lifted his chin and took a deep breath. 'HELP!' he shouted. 'HELP!'

Amita blew the whistle again and again and again.

Then the machine rumbled into movement once more.

Jonathan saw Amita fall to her knees, her head in her hands.

It seemed a million years before anything else happened. First, the sound of a faraway bark, then a small scrabbling sound. Then, suddenly, like the sun coming out, a light shone through the gap. A moving light. Then a flash of colour. It looked like a yellow helmet, but Jonathan couldn't be sure. He saw Amita look up and stretch out her arm. The light shone on her face and he saw tears streaming from her eyes.

A hand came through the gap and reached for her.

'You all right, love?' a deep voice boomed.

'Please tell them to stop digging,' Amita shouted desperately. 'The gas pipe's broken and the electricity cables are sparking. Everything's moving . . . Tell them they've got to stop!'

Jonathan heard a shout, then another further away. Then there was silence. All Jonathan could hear was the sound of his own breath coming out in a huge sigh of relief. He saw Amita turn and point in his direction. 'And there's a little boy . . .'

'It's all right, love,' the voice said. 'We'll have you both out in no time.'

Then there was a loud rumble and stuff began falling. Jonathan heard Amita scream, then the whole world disappeared in a rain of dust.

Jonathan awoke to cold air on his face. He opened his eye. He moved. One leg. The other was encased in some kind of stiff board. The now-familiar pain shot up to his groin. Something was attached to a needle going into his arm. He was lying on a stretcher with someone bending over him. His mum. Tears were streaming down her face and falling on to the red blanket that covered him. His dad stood beside her, his new referee's whistle dangling on a string from his hand. His other hand held Jonathan's so tightly it almost hurt. People milled around, talking. Some were laughing. There were two men in orange waistcoats holding collie dogs on leads. One of the dogs was barking.

Jonathan tried to sit up.

'Where's Amita?' He looked around in panic. There were a load of people standing behind barriers, watching. Anxious-looking people. Some crying. A line of ambulances with their blue, flashing lights, waited . . .

'I'm here.'

Jonathan turned in the direction of the voice. The white bandage round Amita's head looked like a turban. She sat on the kerb. A lady in a sari stood behind her, hugging a tall man with a dark beard.

'There you are, Jonny.' Amita smiled. 'I told you they'd come.'

Acknowledgements

The editor and publishers gratefully acknowledge the following, for permission to reproduce copyright material for this anthology. Every effort has been made to trace copyright holders but in a few cases this has proved impossible. The editor and publishers apologize for these cases of copyright transgression and would like to hear from any copyright holder not acknowledged.

'Barry' by Stephen Bowkett from *Fantastic Space Stories* edited by Tony Bradman, published by Doubleday 1994, copyright © Stephen Bowkett, 1994.

'Gruesome Gran and the Broken Promise' by Trevor Millum from *More of Gary Linekar's Favourite Football Stories,* published by Macmillan 1998, copyright © Trevor Millum, 1998.

'The Computer Ghost' by Terrance Dicks from *Scary Stories* edited by Valerie Bierman, published by Mammoth 1997, copyright © Terrance Dicks, reprinted by permission of Mammoth, an imprint of Egmont Children's Books.

'Barker' by Peter Dickinson from *Guardian Angels* edited by Stephanie Nettell, published by Puffin Books 1988, copyright © Peter Dickinson 1988, reprinted by permission of A.P Watt Ltd.

'Nothing to be Afraid Of' by Jan Mark from *Nothing to be Afraid Of* published by Viking Kestrel 1980, copyright © Jan Mark, 1980, reprinted by permission of David Higham Associates Ltd.

'Maelstrom' by Theresa Breslin from *Amazing Adventure Stories* edited by Tony Bradman, published by Corgi 1994, copyright © Theresa Breslin, 1994, reprinted by permission of the Laura Cecil Literary Agency.

'Baggy Shorts' by Alan MacDonald from *Go For Goal* edited by Wendy Cooling, published by The Orion Publishing Group Ltd 1997, copyright © Alan MacDonald, 1997, reprinted by permission of The Orion Publishing Group Ltd.

'Beauty and the Beast' retold by Adèle Geras from *Beauty and the Beast and Other Stories* published by Hamish Hamilton 1996, copyright © Adèle Geras, 1996.

'Brian and the Brain' by Sara Vogler and Janet Burchett from *Sensational Cyber Stories* edited by

Tony Bradman, published by Doubleday 1997, copyright © Sara Vogler and Janet Burchett, 1997, reproduced by permission of The Agency (London) Ltd. All rights reserved and enquiries to The Agency (London) Ltd, 24 Pottery Lane, London W11 4LZ. Fax: 0207 727 9037.

'A Matter of Time' by Sue Welford from *Amazing Adventure Stories* edited by Tony Bradman, published by Corgi 1993, copyright © Sue Welford, 1993, reprinted by permission of Laurence Pollinger Ltd.